KINGFISHER

SHONA BLASS was born in Glasgow and grew up in London. She wrote stories before she could read, and has been writing them ever since. She studied in Manchester and London. She lives in the New Forest with her husband. *Kingfisher* is the first book in the Kingfisher Series. It is followed by *Eagle Heart* and *Phoenix*.

To find out more visit: www.shonablass.com

KINGFISHER

SHONA BLASS

GOLD CROW BOOKS

First published in 2019 by SilverWood Books
This edition published in 2022 by Gold Crow Books

ISBN 978-1-8382554-4-2 (paperback)
ISBN 978-1-8382554-5-9 (e-book)

Cover design by JD Smith Design

For Paul

CHAPTER 1

'Dominic, wake up.'

I open my eyes and stare through the dark. Flint kneels by my bed, his face in shadow.

'We're in trouble,' he whispers.

My stomach turns. I move quickly to switch on the light but he stops me. He puts a finger to his lips. 'Outside.' He gestures. 'Two trucks. Look like military vehicles.'

Behind him stands my sister Charley. She is dressed and ready to leave.

'They're waiting,' he continues. 'I don't get that. Unless… they're not sure we're here.'

'No.' I shake my head. 'They've found us.' It's the police and MI5. This moment was going to come; they've never stopped searching for us. 'Military vehicles?'

Flint nods. I feel sick. The army is involved.

'We've no way out,' I say. We're in a small cottage. One front door. No back door. Windows too small to climb out of. Fear floods me.

'*What if it's not MI5?*' my sister whispers into my head.

I turn to her. Charley is saying something important, but I can't grasp its meaning, not when I feel this fear.

'*What if it's…*' she continues.

There's a loud bang. The cottage judders as the front door is forced open. There is a charge of footsteps on the stairs. I stop breathing. Flint pales. My sister is close to tears. It only takes seconds for them to reach us. The bedroom door bursts open.

We're staring at a man. Long brown hair, beard, casual clothes and a pistol in his hand. It's pointed at me.

'Up!' he commands. 'Now.' He motions to Charley and Flint. 'All of you. Downstairs!'

I shudder out of bed; my shaking hands fumble with my clothes. Charley and Flint leave first. A woman stands in the hallway, another pistol focused on us.

'Downstairs,' she orders. 'Quickly!'

We reach the kitchen. It's clear there are three of them: two men, one woman, all armed. I didn't think they'd look like this. Dirty clothes, muddy boots, and the smell of rancid sweat. The blokes have long hair; the woman's is short. But they're undercover agents.

We huddle together, arms raised, defenceless. The cottage door is wide open, and a cool breeze blows in. I'm shivering, can't stop my legs shaking. Where did it go wrong? Can't think properly, but it doesn't matter. Result's the same.

A few hours ago, I made love to Mary. We had sex for the first time. Something good finally happened, and I felt safe. But we were not safe. Charley's face is gaunt, her eyes sinking into her head. My cousin Flint, usually so cool and tough, is pale under his dark skin. I've never seen him afraid before, but this is MI5. Nothing can save us now.

We stand there a long time. They must be waiting on someone turning up or issuing a command. Then they'll separate us out. We'll be bundled into those military vehicles, blindfolded and gagged. This may be the last I see of my sister and cousin. My twin sister. We came into the world together, but now we leave it…I clench my teeth against my thoughts. But this is torture – it's how they work: instil dread, leave the victim to contemplate the worst, and let it fester. They will have done this to Dad. I don't want to be hurt, but it's inevitable.

Outside, there is movement. Somebody else is there. A tall shadow comes forward; the one who'll give the order. They step through the doorway. I'm transfixed. They're the arbiter of our fate. He moves slowly into the kitchen then stands tall before us. His body is slim but muscular. A khaki T-shirt is tight across his chest; his trousers are military fatigues. Long dark hair frames his face, but no soldier would have that. His dark eyes spark with energy. His expression is calm. He holds himself very still, yet in that stillness I sense power. But what truly shocks me is I know him, his picture and his place in my imagination. It's Gil Zimmerman, possibly the last person my father spoke to.

'What have we here?' He looks at us and smiles.

I've wanted to find Gil Zimmerman. I should feel relief. He's here. He's not the police or MI5; he's at war with them. But I don't feel relief – I'm just terrified.

'Dominic…Charley…Flint.' He pronounces each of our names slowly. 'At last we meet.'

Silence follows. His eyes shift between us, then come to rest on me.

'Your father's told me a lot about you.' His eyes penetrate mine. 'A brave man, your father…he said you would be too.'

I've never met anyone before who can speak so softly yet with such menace. A gust of cold night air blows in. He turns and closes the door, shutting out the world. He motions to the others to lower their guns.

'Please, take a seat.' He gestures to the kitchen table.

It's hard to move. He sits first and then we obey. It looks like we're about to have a friendly chat; it doesn't feel it.

'I take it you know who I am?' he asks politely. He's one of the most wanted men in the country.

Flint, somehow, manages to reply. 'Gil Zimmerman. You head

the group known as the Disciples. Eco-warriors or, as some would say, you're eco-terrorists.' He sounds defiant. Flint never wanted to seek out Gil, only I did. He feared the security services more, and now he's got the guts to sound defiant. 'MI5,' he continues, 'the police, they'd love to get you. Lock you up and throw away the key.'

Gil watches him closely. 'Correct,' he says coolly, 'but what's important here is the relationship I have with your uncle.'

There are questions I've wanted to ask Gil, things I've imagined saying to him, but now my mind blanks.

'The media are saying…Dad's a traitor,' Charley whispers. She's shaking slightly. 'He was a good man who turned bad, because he involved himself with you.'

'The media would report that,' Gil says. 'It's called propaganda. Your father's a man of conscience. Surely you know that?'

But we are quiet.

'Your father's work was ambitious,' Gil continues. 'It could have led to great things, but, as with so much scientific knowledge, it was going to be misused and for the worst reasons. That's why he came to us…to exercise his conscience,' he says slowly, clearly. 'That's not treachery. He had important information, and if he'd succeeded in giving it to us…if he'd not been arrested…he'd be a hero now.'

I stare at him a long moment. He sounds reasonable, yet there are three people holding guns surrounding us. I speak up. 'Where is he now?' Really, it's the only question. I want my father back.

He turns to me. 'That, Dominic, is a question I can partially answer. The security services have him, although where they're holding him I can't confirm. I'm afraid there is no doubt what they're doing to him. The type of interrogation he's being subjected to is what we call a deep interrogation. He'll tell them everything, that's inevitable, and, as a result, we're in the situation where MI5 are now seeking you.'

My breath catches in my throat.

'Your safety preoccupied your father's thoughts.' Gil's eyes don't move from mine. 'He couldn't tell you about his involvement with us, because it would have been too dangerous, compromising. However, part of the bargain we made…was that I would do everything I could to protect you.'

'Protect us?' I say.

'Yes. I've thought about that a lot. Your need for protection.' He leans forward a little. 'You see, you're sixteen, naïve, and they want to question you for obvious reasons. Your father naturally wanted to protect you from that.' He slows, thoughtful, his fingers tapping the table. 'But…I can't help thinking…that your father was concerned about more than that.'

Bile rises at the back of my throat. It burns.

'Your father was a geneticist,' Gil continues. 'It was his job to alter things at the earliest stages of life. At best, he knew how to make the human body, and animal structures, better, healthier, stronger.' His eyes shift between Charley and me. 'His life's work was enhancing genetic outcomes. So I've asked myself…' He draws out the words; his gaze won't let me go. 'What is it he did to you?'

I stop breathing.

'What is it he did to you? Therefore…what is it we must *really* protect?'

A terrible dread spreads through me. I fear I'm going to crumble. This can't be happening. *He knows, Charley.* My voice is urgent into her head.

'Say nothing,' she answers. *'He doesn't. He can't.'*

'Dad's truly betrayed us.' I despair.

'Say nothing, Dom.'

But all I can think of is my father. Our fates intertwined forever. I stare at Gil Zimmerman and know this is only the beginning.

CHAPTER 2

Six months earlier

Picture it: the home I was happy in when we lived a normal life. When the world was a safe place. A large, red-brick house on a tree-lined street. We had stained glass in the front door with an amazing design – a blazing sun; everyone commented on it. Inside, the rooms were big and airy. The hallway was wide with a varnished wood floor, and we had a summerhouse in the garden. Nicky Salter and I dared to snog in it.

Upstairs, Charley's and my bedrooms were particularly huge. We had a comfy sofa each which could turn into a bed when friends slept over. We had large desks and all the latest tech products. And I had my upright piano and several saxophones.

We were a family. In the living room hung a large photo of Dad, Charley and me. Looking at it, you could see how our faces varied, particularly our noses, but we all had the same blue eyes and mousy coloured hair, although Dad's was flecked with grey, as was his beard and moustache. I wondered how our eyes could be so similar. 'Genes,' Dad said. 'Obviously.'

Mum didn't feature in family shots. She was in the States. My folks got divorced when we were six; we never saw her now, but that was okay. Dad was enough. I never really thought about him being a single parent, because he was always there when we needed him most, like when I fell out of the tree in the park and broke my arm. He was attending a work conference yet, somehow, he got to the hospital before I arrived in the ambulance.

In his study, Dad had a small photo of him with Janice. She was a colleague from work that he went out with, but it wasn't a serious relationship. I think he just liked her company. She was never going to move in or anything like that.

Charley and I knew we were lucky. Dad worked for LifeStar Corporation, and they paid him really well. It meant we had that home and got what we wanted. We didn't go to private school, because the local academy had a great reputation. We lived in a good area. We had friends. I loved life with Dad. I never wanted it to end.

Who was I back then? I had three ambitions for the year: pass my exams in the summer; get Grade 8 on the sax; and find my way into Clare Mint's pants. I knew I'd achieve the first two. I was smart and good at exams. I was going to be a musician. (I play the sax best, piano next and managed Grade 4 on the violin.) As for sex with Clare Mint? No chance, but I liked to believe it was possible. Six months ago, those three things were all I cared about. That changed forever.

It was a Sunday evening in February when it all began. Dad and I were in the basement kitchen. As a family, we spent a lot of time down there. A slight drizzle flecked the windows. It was cold and dark outside; there was a chill in the air. Charley had a heavy period and had gone to bed early. She was dosed up with paracetamol, had a hot water bottle with her, and for all I knew she was fast asleep. Dad and I were alone. He offered me a beer. I liked the fact we were drinking together – a grown-up male thing. He wasn't hung up about stuff like that.

We spoke about school and how things were going. I lied a bit about Clare and made out we were getting serious when in fact she barely spoke to me. Dad nodded and smiled. 'Sounds good,' he said softly.

I opened a packet of crisps and munched on a few. Then something in him darkened. He grew quiet. His face strained. What he said next, I'll never forget.

'Dominic, there is something difficult I have to discuss with you.'

It took me a moment to adjust to how serious he sounded. Suddenly, I worried. Was he going to tell me he was sick? That he had cancer or some horrible disease? I'd no idea how I'd react.

'It's about work,' he continued.

I almost let out a sigh of relief. He wasn't ill.

'It's very important you listen carefully.'

He stopped. In those seconds of silence that followed, I understood we were having a conversation unlike any we'd had before.

'I've done some things I shouldn't have, and there will be consequences.'

I listened. I knew my father's work was secret; we'd learnt long ago never to ask for details, but I had no idea what he was on about now.

'I've been gathering information,' he said slowly. 'I've compiled a file of correspondence that incriminates LifeStar Corporation.'

'What?'

'I'm going to publish information – about LifeStar and the government – that is going to expose a truth people need to know.'

'Dad, what are you on about?'

We were standing in our kitchen; everything around me was familiar, but nothing we were discussing made sense.

'All my life, Dominic, I've tried to do the right thing. I've worked hard in my field, got my PhD, and I taught students successfully at university.'

'Yes.' He was good. He'd done well.

'When I joined LifeStar Corporation, I really believed they were a company trying to make a positive difference to the world.'

Their advert popped into my head. The one they played on television. The voice-over was a breezy female voice. 'In a world of increasing extinctions and the depletion of natural resources, our cutting-edge research into life preservation, the maintenance of ecosystems, and species conservation makes us a unique company. We care about the planet more than our profit.'

'Everybody knows they're a good company, Dad.' I was quick to reassure him.

'I've spent years working on genetic research,' he continued, ignoring my words. 'No, not just years, it's been my life's work.' He shook his head slowly. 'And I've been so blind.'

I gazed into his eyes. My father, usually such a strong and determined man, looked sad and much older.

'I don't understand.' I wanted him to say something different.

'I've been working in a bubble of ignorance, Dom. Can you believe it? A man as intelligent as me working in a bubble of ignorance?' He looked bereft. 'I couldn't have made a bigger mistake. I've known what my research might achieve, positively, but failed to see what it's actually going to be used for.'

His eyes held mine. I felt him willing me to ask the question that should follow such a statement. I swallowed hard, afraid. 'What is it going to be used for?'

'Weapons,' my father whispered, as though the walls had ears. 'The kind of weapon that can inflict untold damage on human beings, yet leave physical structures standing. A weapon that can be targeted at specific ethnic groups and just wipe them out. All that work I've done…and this is what it's come to.'

My head spun. I wanted to put my hands over my ears.

'LifeStar Corporation has a contract with the military,' he continued. 'The research I've been doing is going to be used to develop that weapon. One that an army can release on a town to take out its inhabitants, yet its homes, schools, and buildings will remain standing, ready for immediate occupation.'

'No,' I almost shouted. 'No, Dad. Stop.' I shook my head. 'Stop talking like some computer game or disaster movie. I don't want to hear this.'

'No, Dominic. People aren't going to like what I've got to say, but they need to hear it. They need to know. This can't happen.'

I was standing there, but the ground beneath my feet no longer felt stable.

'You're going to be a whistle-blower?' I said, beginning to understand.

'Yes,' he replied.

My father's going to be a whistle-blower. The words screamed inside my head. I thought of other people who'd been whistle-blowers. They'd had to run, or hide in other countries; they'd been forced to seek immunity elsewhere.

'Dad,' I said, the truth slowly sinking in, 'LifeStar Corporation is a very powerful company…if they're involved with the military, they're not going to let you do this, or…you're going to have to run and hide.'

I felt sick. I could barely believe the conversation we were having.

'I'm not running anywhere,' he told me. 'If they put me on trial, all the better. Even more details will be revealed.'

My eyes were stinging. I was going to lose my father. I couldn't let that happen.

'No, Dad. You can't do this. It's not your responsibility. Whatever's going on, you leave LifeStar, you get another job, but you don't get involved in this. You do not go and break secrets of national security. The p-p-police,' I stuttered, 'MI5,' I stressed, 'will come after you. You cannot do this.'

'I'm going to tell the truth, Dom.'

I felt my lower lip tremble. 'But, Dad, you've got responsibilities. You've got Charley and me.'

His eyes grew very sad. 'Yes,' he said, and I thought he might cry. 'But the responsibility to speak out is greater.'

I shivered; the room felt cold. 'We need to get Charley.' I was struggling. 'Now. She needs to hear this – you can't just tell me alone.'

'No.' He shook his head. 'Charley will get too upset and there are things I need you to know, plans I've made for the two of you, if and when…they come for me.'

'Charley,' I called out her name. I felt desperate. 'Charley!'

There was no reply. She was probably out cold. I considered running upstairs to get her but couldn't. I was rooted to the spot with distress.

'I need you to listen and hear this clearly,' my father continued.

Tears ran down my cheeks; I couldn't control them.

'Don't cry,' he said softly. 'You're sixteen now, and I'm asking you to be a man.'

But I did cry. Not loud sobs, I had to hear what he'd got to say, but still I cried. He told me what he thought would happen. The police would arrest him and he'd disappear for a while into the underground world of the security services. He was prepared for that. He was no longer innocent about the power structures in our society, and it was important I woke up to them too. He spoke about the rebel groups that would pick up on his information. He meant the eco-terrorists and criminal saboteurs discussed on the news. They attacked the buildings and work of the key multinational companies; they were a threat to national security. MI5 and the police sought to destroy them. But now my father believed these groups were right, their cause just.

I felt the blood drain from my face. It was all too much. He stopped talking but not for long.

'I'm sorry this is painful for you,' he said gently. 'All I ever wanted for you and your sister was to give you a good home, somewhere you could feel secure and loved. I'm sorry that security is coming to an end. But I've woken up, Dom. I've opened my eyes, and I have to act.'

He told me where he'd hidden money in the house, his bank card, his PIN. He'd planned it all, what we must do when he didn't return from work. We must leave, avoid the police and any government authority. We mustn't contact our teachers or even Janice.

'You're to go to your Aunt Rena,' he instructed. 'I need you to remember the address. I don't want it written down anywhere.' He explained how we could find her.

Everything was going from bad to worse. We'd met Aunt Rena once, years ago, when she came to stay for a long weekend. It didn't work out. Dad and Rena argued, and her adopted son Flint was trouble. He broke our toys and a speaker on Dad's sound system. We'd not seen them since. The thought that they might be the key to some future security was unbearable. 'No.' I begged, shaking my head.

At last, all words said, my father moved to hug me. We held each other close. I wept. I was losing him. I wanted him to placate me, to apologise, to tell me it wasn't true and that everything would be okay. But those words never came. Instead, I heard his voice hot in my ear.

'You must look after your sister, Dominic. She is…you are… more special than you know.'

CHAPTER 3

I didn't tell Charley what Dad had told me. I knew it was terrible, keeping a truth from her that would eat us both up, but what had happened belonged to Dad and me – a pact sealed between father and son. But I couldn't relate to him either, not like I used to. I hurt too much. Charley picked up on my mood.

'Why are you being so mean to Dad?' she asked, concerned. 'He was talking to you at dinner and you practically ignored him.'

'He's pissed me off,' I told her bluntly.

'What, for days?'

'Yeah, that's right. He's pissed me off for days.' She needed to back off.

'I don't get what's going on with you, Dom. You seem so angry.'

'Well, it's a guy's prerogative.'

She looked upset and I turned away.

'*Tell me,*' she whispered into my head.

We took it for granted we could speak into each other's thoughts; it was a way of communicating that Dad couldn't hear, or our teachers. And I almost told her then, when she asked me like that, but the pain of the truth was more than I could say.

'It's between Dad and me, Charley,' I answered aloud. 'Just something between the two of us.'

Every day I came home from school, I wondered if this would be the evening he didn't return from work. Yet each night he did, and I started to think that maybe it wouldn't happen. His confession in the kitchen had been something he'd had to get off his chest, but now he'd changed his mind. Janice came round Friday night and spent the weekend with us. Things were relaxed; we all went out to a film together and then for a meal. On Monday, life was as regular as ever. On Tuesday evening, I had a sax lesson. It was the last lesson I'd ever have. As I was taking down my saxophone, talking to my teacher, I saw Charley looking through the classroom door window. She was distraught. She burst into the room.

'Dominic, you've got to come. Now!' Her eyes welled up.

I knew what I'd been hoping we could escape had arrived. I said goodbye to my teacher, and Charley and I ran down the corridor together.

'The house has been broken into.' Charley was almost breathless. 'There's blood on the doorstep, I couldn't go in. I think something terrible has happened.'

'*It has*,' my thoughts whispered. She turned to me in anguish.

When we got back, we stood before our home. Neither of us was ready to go in. The place had been wrecked. The front door was ajar; it had been forced open and looked too damaged to shut properly. The curtains upstairs were closed and the plants in the front garden trampled on. There were drops of blood on the doorstep. I felt sick. All of it confirmed there had been a struggle.

Eventually, I dared to push the front door open. The hallway was a mess. Dad's bike lay upturned on the wooden flooring. Shoes and boots we kept neatly at the door had been kicked about. Mail had been ripped up, the remains scattered like unholy confetti.

'Dad,' I called out, but I knew there would be no answer.

'Dad!' Charley shouted.

There was no reply – only silence. We walked, dazed, from room to room. Each one had been ransacked: drawers opened and emptied, their contents thrown randomly on the floor. The kitchen was a wreck of dispersed utensils, food thrown from cupboards; even a bag of flour had been emptied, its white dust coating the cooker. In the bathrooms, tops had been broken off shampoo and shower gel bottles as though something might have been hidden inside. Dad's computer, and all the files he kept in his study, were gone. They'd stripped the room.

We walked slowly into our bedrooms. They'd opened the cupboards and emptied the drawers there too. Charley's underwear lay exposed on the floor. They'd upturned our dirty washing sacks, ripped books off our shelves, and dug a packet of condoms out from under my bed. Neither of us could speak; we were too distressed. Our home had been violated.

'Those bastards,' I finally muttered.

Charley was frozen, her face ashen. I felt the blood drain from my limbs; I was going to be sick. I ran to the bathroom. Lunch had been eaten hours ago but it still found its way back up. Shaking, I splashed cold water on my face. When I returned to the hallway, Charley still stood there; she didn't move. We were quiet for a time.

'There's something I need to tell you,' I whispered. I told her everything Dad had said. The words tasted like blood in my mouth. She cried.

'I don't know if I'll ever forgive you,' she hiccupped, 'for not telling me before.'

She didn't say anything else. She turned from me and walked into her room. It was hard to breathe; my throat burnt. I watched her curl up on her bed and hug her large toy rabbit. She had used that bunny for comfort since she was a child.

I went into my room and slammed the door shut. Pain screamed in my ears. Our father had gone. Our home was wrecked. He'd forced a piece of knowledge between us and left us in this situation. None of it should have happened. I hated him.

At some point, I must have fallen asleep on the floor, because when I woke it was dark outside. I checked my watch; it was nine thirty. I'd been out for hours. Through the haze of darkness, my eyes focused on Charley. She was standing still against the wall.

'I hate what's happened,' she whispered.

'*Me too,*' I said into her head. I knew she was saying she didn't hate me.

'Why didn't Dad tell me?' She was close to tears. 'I could've stopped him.' She shook her head. 'And…he didn't let me say goodbye.'

I had to close my eyes; it all hurt so much. I tried to speak. 'I think…Nothing was going to stop him, Charley. His mind was made up. He didn't tell you because he said you'd get too upset.'

'Upset?' she said, anguished. 'And weren't you upset, Dom?'

'I've been mad at him for weeks,' I shouted. 'I am upset!'

We stopped. We couldn't argue. I took a few deep breaths; we had to stay calm.

Charley eventually spoke into my head. '*He's left me something.*'

She walked towards me. I realised she was still holding her toy bunny. She bent down low beside me and guided my hand to the seam on the rabbit's back. Halfway down, the stitching appeared to have been ripped slightly. Something sharp was against my fingers. I withdrew my hand, and from the gap in the seam she pulled out a small piece of paper. Neither of us spoke. She flattened it out. Dad's writing was clear. There was a single word to read. 'KINGFISHER.'

'*What does it mean?*' she asked.

'*I don't know,*' I replied silently.

I glanced round the room. Somewhere, I had an old British bird book. It had been bought for me years ago although I'd rarely looked at it. Now it was torn in two, but I picked up the halves and leafed through it.

'*Alcedo atthis*.' I read its Latin name. '"The kingfisher lives on the banks of rivers and streams. Its nests are well hidden and they are often difficult to see. However, their distinctive luminous blue feathers are the defining feature by which you can recognise them as they dive down for their prey."'

'I don't think I've ever seen one,' said Charley.

'No…and Dad was no birdwatcher.'

We looked at each other. It made no sense. Why would Dad leave the name of a bird, one we'd never even seen, stuffed into the back of Charley's rabbit? Everything about the act implied it was important: the covert hiding of paper, the single scribbled word. But if it was code, we'd no idea what it was for.

After a while, I spoke. 'We need to get out of here.' I feared we were more vulnerable than we realised.

'I don't want to go to Aunt Rena's,' Charley said. 'I don't think we should go there.'

'We must,' I said. 'There's a letter there from Dad. I don't know why he had to leave it with her, but he has. We'll go, find her, get the letter and then move on.' I had no desire to spend time with Rena either.

'Will Flint be there?' Charley asked.

I shrugged. 'Possibly.'

She grimaced. Then we both got our rucksacks and started to stuff them with the things we thought we'd need most. A few changes of clothing, underwear, a toothbrush and toothpaste.

'We'll be back in a few days, won't we?' Charley lugged her rucksack into my room. I couldn't reply because I didn't want to lie.

We made the decision to stay in the house overnight then leave at five when the transport system kicked into action. We ate a meal of biscuits and cheese, cereal and ice cream. It didn't feel home anymore. We slept on top of our beds, clothes on. Early next morning, I took a long hot shower, aware it would probably be my last for some time. We pulled our rucksacks onto our backs and left. I had a money belt strapped round my waist which contained the cash from Dad's room; he'd hidden it beneath a floorboard. I withdrew as much money as I could from several cash machines. We weren't going to starve; he'd left us a lot. Then we walked to the nearest Underground station and took the quickest route out of London.

CHAPTER 4

Rena and Flint were difficult to find. We travelled all day by tube, two trains and a bus. Eventually, we reached a village full of quaint cottages and well-kept houses. But they didn't live there – no such luck. Instead, we trekked on until we found two boggy fields with mobile homes and caravans. The inhabitants' eyes followed us suspiciously as we walked between them. Dogs barked, and one Staffordshire bull terrier looked about to attack. Charley drew closer, her body jostling against mine. I decided I wouldn't stop to ask which home was Rena's. We needed to look like we knew what we were doing.

In the end, I recognised Flint sitting outside a mobile home. It was nine years since we'd seen him, but I had no doubt who it was with his dark skin and loose afro hair. He had tattoos now; a mix of Celtic and tribal-looking patterns covered both his arms.

'Flint?' I tried to sound relaxed.

Flint raised his eyebrows and gave a half smile. Without saying a word, he indicated we should go inside. I raised my hand to knock on the door, but it opened. An older woman, with some resemblance to Dad, stood before us. She was shorter and stockier than Dad, but had the same blue eyes and grey in her hair.

'Aunt Rena,' I said politely.

'Oh, dear.' She sighed. 'I was hoping I wouldn't see you. It means Brian's in trouble.' We all paused a moment on the threshold. I was surprised; even her voice was like Dad's, although where she lived was clearly very different.

'You'd better come in,' she said, drawing back from the door.

We sat down around a small white plastic table that filled Rena's kitchen and half the living room. She moved to put the kettle on. Flint stepped inside, closing the door behind him. He stood there silent, his eyes not moving from us. Their home was confining – it felt claustrophobic. I wasn't comfortable. Turning to Charley, I noticed her lower lip tremble.

'Did it take you long to get here?' Rena asked, coming to the table with mugs of tea. I noticed her hands; the skin was rough.

'A while,' I replied. Charley was shrinking into herself. She wasn't ready to talk.

'When did the police get him?' Rena queried bluntly. She opened a packet of dry-looking biscuits. I was hungry but didn't eat.

'Yesterday,' I told her. I wondered how much she knew. 'Did Dad tell you what he was involved in?'

'A bit,' she said. 'To be honest, I didn't want to know. I've got enough problems of my own.'

I couldn't tell if she was being hostile or just matter-of-fact. Anyway, she didn't know us. Why should she care? Flint shifted where he stood. He didn't say a word.

'Dad said he left something for us with you.' I decided to get to the point. I didn't want to stay there. 'An envelope.'

'He left a letter,' Rena said slowly. She probably thought I was being rude. She got up, opened one of the drawers in her small kitchen and withdrew an A5 envelope. She handed it to me. 'CHARLEY AND DOMINIC'. Dad's writing was clear across the top. The lip at the back was stuffed inside rather than sealed down.

'Have you read it?' I asked, sensing its contents were not as private as they should have been.

Flint gave a cough. My eyes darted to him. His gaze didn't shift.

'It's for you, not for me,' said Rena, but that didn't answer the question.

'We need to take time to read this,' I said, wondering how we'd get some privacy.

'Of course.' She nodded. There was a brief silence between us. 'But…you both look tired and hungry. Let's eat first. That won't make easy reading.'

Now I was convinced she'd read it.

'You'll both be safe here for a while.' She tried to smile.

I looked into her eyes. Maybe she wasn't hostile, but she was tough.

'Brian…your father…has been good to me over the years,' she continued, her voice softer. 'And to Flint, always helping to provide for Flint. I owe him. You're welcome here.'

'Thank you,' I replied. But I was shocked. I had no idea my father had been in regular contact with Rena, or that he'd provided for Flint.

'You'll never fit us all in here,' Charley blurted out. It was the first thing she'd said. I could have kicked her.

Rena smiled. 'Don't you worry. This place is bigger than it looks. We've two bedrooms and a couch there that can be used as a bed. Flint won't mind.'

We were quiet. We didn't know one another and we lived in different worlds. It wasn't clear what else we might say. Rena boiled up a big pan of pasta and poured on a couple of tins of meat sauce. It was something our father would never do. He took pride in his cooking. He'd have made a fresh sauce, added extra vegetables and used organic meat. She put a plate of white sliced bread on the table and a tub of cheap margarine. Dad would have gone for wholemeal bread and butter.

As the plates of food were put before us, Charley spoke to me silently. *I don't think I can eat this.*

'*Well, you'll have to,*' I instructed, equally silent. '*This is what we've got so this is what we'll eat.*' I thanked Rena and tucked in, ravenous.

Charley picked up her fork and slowly twizzled some of the spaghetti around it. She put it to her mouth and chewed.

'You alright, love?' Rena asked, watching her.

Charley nodded, yes, and attempted to smile. She didn't do it very well.

'I guess this has been pretty hard for you,' Rena said softly.

Charley nodded again. Then she was crying, sobbing over her spaghetti. I put down my fork, closed my eyes and put my hands over my face. I couldn't make this better.

'Alright, dear,' said Rena, getting up and moving to her. She got Charley to stand then hugged her. 'You're going to be alright,' she repeated, rocking Charley gently to and fro.

I glanced over at Flint. He had stopped eating to watch the mini drama. We caught each other's eyes and shared a brief moment of male solidarity. Neither of us belonged there. We continued eating while Rena plied my sister with tissues. Eventually, she sat down.

'I'm sorry,' said Charley, 'but I don't think I can eat. I'm too tired.' She continued to wipe tears from her eyes.

Rena signalled to Flint to show Charley where she could rest. She looked exhausted. There were two bedrooms beyond the kitchen, and Flint was giving us his. Charley closed the door quietly behind her. Flint sat down again and we continued eating without talking. Rena put on the radio and tutted now and then at the news.

After dinner, I sat a while in silence as Rena cleared up. I felt awkward, itching to get away. Flint sat outside smoking. It was dark but it wasn't too cold. I decided to join him.

'Cigarette?' he offered. He had a tin of tobacco and Rizla paper.

'No thanks.' I shook my head.

'You don't smoke.' He smiled. 'Drink?'

'Sometimes,' I answered.

'Screw?'

'Sometimes,' I lied. He chuckled; I don't lie well.

'Didn't think so.' He looked at me a long moment. 'You think you're better than everybody else, don't you? 'Cause that's what I remember you was like.'

'Really?' I wasn't sure what to say, but decided on the truth. 'I remember you as spoilt. Never heard the word "no".'

He smiled at me again. 'Still am, sometimes. 'Specially with Rena.' He indicated the ground beside him. 'Sit down.'

I wasn't sure I wanted to join him, but there wasn't anywhere else to go. We sat a while, quietly, the distinctive smell of his roll-up wafting under my nose.

'You're my only cousins,' Flint eventually continued.

'Maybe that's a good thing. You might not like having cousins.' After all, we'd imposed ourselves on him.

'Or I might,' he said softly.

I looked at him; we were communicating, but I wasn't sure what we were really saying.

'Charley's pretty,' he said, 'when she's not crying.'

I turned away. I wasn't sure how I felt about him noticing her like that. 'I guess.' I shrugged.

'She got a boyfriend?'

I shook my head, no.

'Hmm, I thought she'd have some nice little posh boy following her around.'

'No,' I said firmly. 'There are no nice little posh boys in our lives.'

'Okay. Stay cool.'

I stared through the dark into the distance. This place was grim. A couple of young kids were screaming in their play. I saw a dog taking a shit in the walkway. The smell of Flint's cigarette was too strong. I stood up.

'I'm going in to read that letter.'

'No, you're not,' Flint said, without turning to me. 'Rena's put it away. You can get it tomorrow.'

A flash of rage shot through me. How dare they keep that letter from us?

Flint turned to me, his expression serious. 'You really don't want to read that tonight.'

I realised he'd read it too. Rena and Flint, they had both read it. We had no privacy.

'If I were you,' he said gently, 'I wouldn't want to ever read that letter.'

Chapter 5

Flint was right. It was a letter you'd never want to read. The next day, Charley and I found a quiet spot at the edge of the campsite. Alone, we read what my father had to say.

My dearest Charley and Dominic,

If you are holding this letter, then what I have feared would happen has taken place. Your Aunt Rena agreed to keep it safe. Please trust her, she is probably the only person at present you can.

I wish things were different, and the mistakes I have made in my life were only my own and might never affect you. I am sorry that is not the case, and now I cannot protect you from the truth.

I am committed to making amends for the work I've been involved in, trying in some way to alter the future's possibilities. I am not unafraid. I know what those in power, and the security services, are likely to do to me for exposing LifeStar's actions. I am sure that, during my interrogation, I will tell them everything. They will get the information they want from me and more. I'm neither brave nor stupid. I understand the consequences of my actions. What is important now is that you know the truth about yourselves. You need to understand why you can never go home. This is the hardest thing I have ever had to write.

For a long time before you were born, your mother and I were trying for a baby. Nobody could identify the problem stopping your mother getting pregnant, but we were advised to try IVF. You were the result. I have never told you this before, although there is nothing unusual or exceptional about IVF these days. I never spoke of it, because I did something I never should have. I applied my work to the fertilised embryos.

There is a vanity in parents, a great desire for our children to somehow be exceptional, a cut above the rest. Any parent who tells you otherwise is lying. I had isolated genes at work that I believed would make you just such exceptions. The doctor involved in our IVF was fascinated. He agreed to collude with my 'gene therapy'. It wasn't legal, but I felt it was right.

You were born, two wonderful, healthy children, and I have always loved you for who you are. That has taught me the greatest lesson; you are exceptional because I love you, and you are mine, not because of anything I could add to your abilities.

But the truth of what I've done is going to come out. Then the authorities will want to find you, and you cannot let them get you. They will see you as specimens to be experimented on. They will want to figure out what's been done to you, and then, no doubt, how they might use you. You must understand how serious this is. Capture threatens your lives and, more than anything, I want you to live and I want you to thrive.

For a long time, I stopped myself taking action against LifeStar in order to protect you. But you are sixteen now and ultimately I could delay no more; the truth about LifeStar must to be told. I have taken what measures I can to ensure your safety.

You must stay with Rena for a while. We have had limited contact over the years, and her lifestyle means she has little contact with the authorities. Any surveillance is unlikely to focus on her immediately. This information about you will not be the first they'll hear from me or want to pursue. I have done worse. But in time they'll want to find you. Be assured, they will come for you. I cannot advise what you do then except keep moving, running, trusting only where it is safe. I have faith that you can do that.

I have tried to contemplate the impact of these truths on you. I have always wanted to be a good father, but with these actions I know I have failed you, and caused you suffering. It pains me deeply to know I have hurt the two people in the world I most want to avoid hurting.

I beg your forgiveness, if you can grant it. I hope, one day, you will find the ability to remember me well.

I will love you, always.

Charley and I could neither move nor speak. The letter was written in our father's hand, but what he'd done was not him – not the father we knew. Our whole lives had suddenly become something else: who we thought we were; the home we'd grown up in; all we had known. Nothing had been what it seemed. Our father had kept a secret from us, one that went to the core of our beings.

My body was shaking involuntarily; I was in shock. Charley was ghostly white, as though someone had slit her wrists and let the blood drain out.

'*What does this mean?*' She couldn't speak aloud, only into my thoughts.

'*Our lives are finished,*' I responded, my voice equally trapped. '*Are we mutants?*'

I couldn't look at her. *'Something like that.'*

We were quiet for a long time. Charley started crying beside me. I had never seen her cry so much as over the last few days. It was as if someone had died. And they had. We had died, and our father to us. I looked at the letter again. It felt cold in my hands. It might be his last will and testament. He spoke of love, but what he had done was not love.

'He's betrayed us,' I said, bereft.

Charley tried to speak through whoops of crying. 'He doesn't say what he did to us. What genes he played with.'

'No,' I said, breathing hard.

Was that his final act of cruelty? To leave us not knowing. Or was he trying to protect us from another truth that might be even harder to bear? We were silent, trying to take in what we'd read.

The sun shifted position in the sky; time passed, but it didn't move for us. Charley exhausted herself crying. I felt sick, then numb.

'What are we going to do, Dom?' Charley eventually whispered.

'I don't know.'

'We'll never be able to go home.'

'No.' There was a lump in my throat so large it hurt.

In the distance, I saw Flint coming towards us. He approached slowly, his expression serious. 'Rena says you should come back now.' He stood by us. 'She's worried about you.'

I looked up into his face, his dark eyes observing us closely. Rena was worried; the words didn't make sense. We were all caught up in something, and nothing made sense anymore.

Flint put out a hand to help Charley up. After a pause, she took it and stood. She looked shell-shocked. Her eyes were vacant. I realised I was shaking again. I watched her move with Flint back towards the caravan. I was suddenly full of rage, so powerful and strong I thought I'd start screaming. I'd scream and not be able to stop. I bit my lower lip until I could taste the metallic flavour of my own blood. I stayed there a long time, hoping I'd explode, disintegrate, break into a hundred thousand pieces, anything that would stop me feeling this desolate.

Later, I picked myself up and walked back to Rena's. I was tired and hungry. Flint was sitting outside again, smoking. He took a long drag on his cigarette.

'Where's Charley?' I asked, although the answer was obvious.

'Inside,' he replied, 'talking with Rena.' He shrugged; he wasn't going to get involved.

I didn't want to go inside. I didn't want to speak to Rena. 'I hate my father,' I told him bluntly.

He looked at me a long moment. 'Hmm. I don't reckon I'd like someone messing with me either.' At least he got what I was saying. 'But hey, you might have been messed with in a good way, you just don't know.'

I wasn't ready to consider that possibility.

'Can we be friends, Flint?' I asked, wondering. It wasn't what I'd wanted the night before, but I was a different person now. 'I'd…I'd like a friend.'

He smiled softly. 'Let's get out of here,' he offered, standing.

CHAPTER 6

We walked into the village. Flint knew the off-licence well and said they wouldn't query my age. He told me what to do. I was to buy a six pack of beer, and he would get us something stronger. I should take my time paying and keep the sales assistant distracted. I chatted briefly making my purchase until Flint walked out the door. I took my change off the counter and left. Further down the road, Flint produced a large bottle of whisky from inside his jacket.

'Shit, Flint,' I said, horrified and impressed. 'Don't you worry you'll get caught?'

He tutted at me as though I was stupid. 'I know what I'm doing. If I was gonna get caught, I'd leave it.'

He didn't seem remotely bothered he'd just committed a crime. And I was an accomplice.

We went and sat on a bench in a deserted children's playground. I opened a can of beer and gulped it down. I'd been slightly drunk before, but it was nothing to what I intended now. I drank another can and burped loudly, the liquid heavy in my stomach.

'That,' said Flint, after I commented on it, 'is why I love spirits.'

He unscrewed the whisky bottle, took a long swig from it then passed it to me. I felt the whisky burn its way down my throat, setting my insides alight.

'Jesus,' I said, and smelt the alcohol on my breath.

Flint laughed beside me, shaking his head, amused. 'Have you got a lot to learn.'

I passed the bottle to him, but he just pushed it back. 'Don't stop now.'

I drank some more, then he took it. He swallowed it down easily. We were quiet for a while.

'I hate my father.' I just couldn't keep the words down.

'Least you've had one,' Flint said matter-of-factly. 'I look at you, and you ain't done so badly.'

That made me angry, but then it passed. The alcohol was taking effect. 'You're adopted, right?' I asked carefully. 'So…you've never met your dad.'

'I'm adopted,' he answered, watching me a moment. 'I remember Frank,' he said, 'when I was very young.' Frank, I knew, had been Rena's husband. 'But, obviously, he's dead now, so really…I've no dad.'

'That's kind of hard.'

He shrugged. 'I don't know. Can't see no point getting upset about something you can't change.'

I thought about that. 'Well, I would.' I decided to speak my mind. 'If I was you, Flint, I'd have to try and trace my dad. If I was adopted, I'd want to know who my father was. That would really bug me.'

'Dom,' he said, a smile on his face, 'you *do* know who your father is, and it *really bugs* you.'

I couldn't respond to that; my tongue felt slightly numb. Flint laughed. What we'd said wasn't funny, but I started laughing too. We were getting drunk. Flint stood up and walked towards the roundabout. He began to spin it and then jumped on. Only he didn't make it; his legs tangled under him. I laughed louder.

He sat on one of the swings. I went over and joined him. I held onto the chains the swing was hanging from and leaned back. The moon was huge above.

'I think it's a full moon,' I said. 'Perhaps I'll discover I'm a werewolf.'

'Let's hope so. Nothing much happens round here.'

'Ah oooh!' I howled.

'Ah oooh!' he replied, and it sent a shiver down my spine.

'That sounded real.'

He smiled and began to swing back and forth. He kept his eyes on the moon, and we were quiet for a while.

He eventually spoke, bringing his swing to a halt. 'You know, the Native American people are some of the most oppressed people in the world.'

It was the last thing I expected him to say.

'You know why?' he said, gesturing at the sky. 'Because when they looked at the moon, they knew it had spirit. And the sun and the earth. And white man couldn't bear that.'

'No?' I said, wondering where Flint had got this from.

'No. White man can't bear spirit in the world. He likes rules and laws and science, thinking he's above such primitive things as spirit. White men like your dad and all those suckers working for companies like LifeStar Corporation.' He shook his head disapprovingly. 'Big mistake,' he said, but then smiled anyway.

I knew I was drunk. Either the swing was moving below me or the sky above.

'And even though they were defeated,' Flint continued, drawing his swing back, 'the native tribes of America, they were warriors. They were tough, tough warriors.' He swung forward and took a leap. He landed well on both feet.

'Warriors.' I burped. I considered standing but decided against it. 'What tribe are we from, Flint?' It seemed right to continue the theme.

'You,' said Flint, turning to me, 'are from pathetic little white boy tribe, but me, I'm something else. I reckon I've Native American blood in me. I feel it.'

I gazed at him. 'Flint, that's crazy. There's no way you can be Native American.'

'What do you know?' he challenged. 'You never met my father, so how do you know?'

'Well,' I said, trying not to slur my words. 'It's kind of obvious, when I look at you, that your dad, or your mum, was black.'

Flint shook his head. 'Shit, Dom. You lack imagination. I know what I feel in my blood. And anyway, who says a man can't be both black and Native American?' He opened his arms wide, questioning me.

Was this what happened when you didn't know your father? You made stuff up?

'I got Native American blood in me,' Flint insisted, swaying slightly. 'Nobody tells me who I am, but me.'

I was too gone to argue. Instead, I laughed again. Who cared if Flint had some crazy story to explain himself? I liked him anyway. Then the earth seemed to be getting closer. I tumbled from the swing and rolled over onto my back.

'Would I make a good warrior?' I asked, wondering if I was going to be sick. I figured a warrior could drink whisky without being sick.

'Hell, no, you wouldn't,' he said, 'but you might just have to become one anyway, and if the police come for you…well…yeah.'

I didn't want to think about that. From where I lay, Flint's head was partially eclipsing the moon. He kept staring down at me. 'You know,' he continued, 'right now, I can see how you look like Charley.'

I closed my eyes. There was movement behind them. 'She's my twin sister. Who else would I look like?'

'Thing is, she's pretty. That's okay in a girl, but not in a guy.'

'Pretty?' Nobody had ever called me that before.

'Yeah. She's pretty. I like her.'

'Forget it. She's not going to like you. You don't know Charley.'

Flint shook his head, grinning. 'She will. When she gets to know me, she'll like me.'

He had no chance with Charley. The one guy she'd dated (and not even that was for long) went to a private school and wanted to be an astrophysicist.

'Anyway,' he said, 'you should get up now. All this talk of sex is making me want some.'

We hadn't mentioned sex once, had we? I rolled over and struggled to stand. We started back towards the caravan park. I staggered more than walked, leaning alternately against Flint and then the hedgerow. He stopped periodically to help me regain my balance. Halfway home, Flint unzipped his flies and took a slash. I joined him. The piss kept coming, and I started to fall into a thorny bush.

'Don't prick your prick, man.' Flint caught me.

We dissolved into laughter. I was glad for Flint. Pissing and laughing at the same time was too demanding.

When we reached the caravan site, Flint sauntered over to one of the smaller homes. He knocked on the door. There was no reply.

'Ange,' he called out gently. 'It's me, Flint.' He paused. 'I'm sorry I haven't been for a while.'

Still, there was no reply. I shivered. I wanted to get back.

'Ange,' Flint called louder.

A marmalade cat walked out of the shadow; it brushed against Flint's leg. 'She's out.' He sighed with disappointment, then bent down and ruffled the cat's fur. 'Hey, Titanic.'

'Titanic?' I'd never heard a more inappropriate name.

Flint chuckled and the cat disappeared through a flap in the caravan door.

He turned to me. 'Let's get you home.' We continued walking haphazardly. 'Shame Ange wasn't in.' He shook his head. 'Now I got to take you back a virgin.'

CHAPTER 7

We reached Rena's and I crashed through the caravan, waking both her and Charley. I vomited down the toilet, then spent hours hugging the bathroom floor. The next morning, I crawled back into the bedroom. Charley was furious with me.

Her voice scratched my eardrums. 'You went with Flint and left me. But I was upset too, Dom. You went with him, got pissed and…I don't know, you probably got up to worse than that. Don't think I don't know what Flint's about.' She paused but not for long. 'How could you, Dom? You betrayed me.'

I'd left her alone after reading that letter, the worst letter we could have read. I fumbled over my words, struggling to excuse myself, trying to explain Flint wasn't as bad as she thought, but I knew I didn't sound convincing.

My head throbbed as if an anvil was banging inside it, and my mouth was parched. As the effects of the alcohol began to wear off, a hollow feeling opened up inside. But there was no time to wallow in my emotions. Rena had left her morning paper on the kitchen table. Dad's picture was on the front page. I stared at his image through bleary eyes. Charley gasped. The headline was brutal: 'TRAITOR.'

The report was a garbled mix of truth and lies. Brian Minster, brilliant scientist with so much to give, was arrested on suspicion of involvement with the eco-terrorist group the Disciples. The authorities were still trying to piece the story together, but it was feared he'd already released highly sensitive information. They were hoping the damage could be limited, but security at a number of key installations had been increased. LifeStar Corporation was mentioned only once. The theme of the story was national security.

'No,' Charley wailed.

The report was sprinkled with lies about his sex life too – tabloid entertainment. He'd had affairs with his best students, and Janice was quoted confessing to his strange habits in bed. It was all proof he couldn't be trusted. It was what a traitor did.

'That's not Dad,' I said, growing increasingly upset. For the first time since I'd read his letter, I felt a wave of protectiveness towards him.

In the days that followed, more reports appeared in the media. They all told a similar story. A few mentioned that Brian Minster had two children the authorities would like to interview. But they didn't say more than that, not about us. Still, Rena decided she wasn't taking any chances. She banned us from straying far from the caravan, from using our phones or doing anything that might mean we could be traced.

'But we'll miss our exams,' Charley protested. 'We have to find a way to sit our exams.' We were all together in the kitchen.

Rena shrugged. 'There is no way. You've got to forget about school…at least for now.'

'No, you don't understand. We're not like Flint,' Charley said deliberately, clearly, as though Rena had trouble hearing. 'We were doing well at school. And if we don't sit those exams, people will think we're stupid, or that we flunked out.'

I glanced at Flint, but he didn't seem offended.

'Charley,' Rena said softly, 'I don't care what anybody thinks.

All I'm concerned about it your safety, and while you're in my home, which you are, you'll do as I say.'

'I could have got As,' Charley said, distressed. 'How am I ever meant to get into medical school now?' She stormed out of the kitchen and into our room, slamming the door behind her.

I couldn't speak; I was just as upset. How was I meant to be a musician? Peter James and I had been on the verge of taking our jazz band out on gigs. But that was when we had a future.

Days passed. As the reality of our situation sank in, my mood darkened. Charley and I lounged around the kitchen for long hours, at a loss for what to do. Neither of us wanted to be there, but there was no alternative. We were paying a high price for Dad's actions. Flint, however, had other plans.

'Not interrupting anything, am I?' he said, opening the caravan door.

It was late afternoon, and his sudden presence felt noisy and intrusive. He was interrupting our private misery.

'Don't look sad.' He strode past us to open one of the kitchen cupboards and took out a saucer. 'Charley,' he turned to her, 'I've got something for you.'

He poured some milk into the saucer then put it on the table near her. From inside his jacket, he produced a small bundle of fur and claw: a kitten. He held it out to her, and my sister's sullen face brightened. 'That's to make up for the night we went drinking,' he said softly. 'We shouldn't have left you behind.'

I'd never heard anyone lie so sincerely. I shook my head gently, incredulous. What would Charley have made of Ange?

The kitten mewed and Charley took it in her hands. Her face opened into an expression of joy; her mood transformed. She cuddled it. I turned to my cousin. His eyes didn't move from her.

I'd completely underestimated him.

Charley became inseparable from her kitten. She retreated into a private world where the cat was her comfort. Stroking it was simple, easy, a warm hand on soft fur. She loved it when there was so little else to like.

One warm, balmy evening, I sat outside with Flint. He lit a cigarette and watched my sister, feet away. She was trying to train the kitten to come when called and to turn a circle.

'Jesus, she wants that cat to do circus tricks,' I said disparagingly, but really I was jealous of how much she cared for it.

'Yeah,' Flint said, 'and she might succeed.'

Flint's desire for my sister was increasingly obvious. Charley glanced over and smiled. 'Look, she's beginning to get it.'

Flint smiled back and held her gaze for too long.

I eventually spoke, softly. 'She's only sixteen, and my sister. Don't even think about it.' I wasn't really threatening him, just letting him know how I felt.

He turned to me. 'What do you think I'm going to do to her?' he asked slowly and without humour.

I was tongue-tied. What did I think was happening?

'She's innocent, Flint,' I said, 'and you're not. I know you find her attractive, but please, back off.'

'What do you think I'm going to do to her?' he repeated, bemused.

I felt myself blush, confused. She was my sister; he was my cousin. Nothing could happen between them. It wasn't right. 'I feel protective towards her,' I insisted.

I don't know what Flint would have said next, because then something happened that captured all our attentions. Charley's cat wasn't the only animal in the area. There were dogs, and of all of them Jimmy's Staffie (as we called him) was the one to fear most.

He was a menace; I was always expecting him to bite. Now, he was careering towards us. It wasn't something we hadn't seen before, he'd suddenly charge here and there, only this time Charley and her kitten were before him.

Flint and I registered what was going to happen before he actually attacked. We knew it, but there was nothing we could do to stop it. And it was suddenly too dangerous for Charley to pick up the kitten. The dog's stocky body and vicious mouth were fast upon the cat. It screeched horribly for an animal so small as the dog flung it from side to side. The kitten became still in its mouth.

Flint rose quickly, moving to kick the dog and swearing it off. The Staffie dropped the kitten, looked down at its handiwork, then scampered away. My sister's face paled. The cat, which had only a few moments before been a source of such happiness, was dead. She picked up the small mass of fur and blood.

'Shit,' Flint said, upset.

Charley held the kitten close, tucking it between her shoulder and chin as she liked to do when it was alive. I couldn't speak. Everything had become impossible. Not even something as simple as a kitten, or the joy it gave her, seemed able to survive.

'Charley,' I said, standing, wanting to make something better. I moved closer but the cat was lifeless against her, its little head twisted. We were quiet. Charley began to cry. At first it was soft, but then it started to crescendo. Her sobbing moved through me. Tears not just for the kitten, but for everything we'd lost.

I touched her arm. 'We should bury it.' I looked over at Flint, who nodded in agreement.

We moved a little way into the woodland at the back of the caravan site, and Flint dug a hole. There seemed nothing we could say, not for comfort; we just had to put the small body in the ground and cover it over. But Charley wouldn't let go. She continued to sob and kiss the kitten, as though somehow she could breathe it back to life. I was surprised at Flint's patience. He appeared in no hurry, although I felt agitated. It was time to bury the animal, just as I knew, in some way, we had to bury our past. Eventually, my sister moved to put the kitten in the ground. As she lowered it, it mewed. She stopped. We listened; it mewed again.

'She's alive,' she whispered.

Flint and I looked at each other. Both of us knew the cat had been dead. We moved closer. It struggled in Charley's hands, but it was alive.

'She heard me, and she's alive.' Her eyes brightened. She stood up and started to walk back towards the caravan park. Flint and I watched her, silent and still.

'She's going to nurse it now,' I said, incredulous.

Flint didn't respond immediately. 'Dominic, it was dead.'

My head was spinning. 'No, we must have been mistaken.'

'It was dead,' Flint repeated.

I felt my heart pounding in my chest. Something had happened I was struggling to comprehend. I turned to Flint. 'We both know what we saw,' I said, breathy, as though I'd been exerting myself. 'But let's not mention it, let's never talk of it again.'

Flint held my gaze.

My heart beat so wildly, I feared it would burst. I didn't want to believe what I'd seen. 'We must forget it,' I insisted.

Flint wouldn't reply. He pushed past me, and followed the path my sister had taken back to Rena's. The world began to spin. I stepped back quickly to steady myself, but my foot fell into the burial hole. My ankle crunched and I gasped in pain. Looking ahead, I could no longer see Charley or Flint. I was alone.

*

Whatever happened that day, it was quickly forgotten; our photos were suddenly in the papers. We'd been at Rena's for weeks and never fully accepted it was the lull before the storm. But now they had printed old school shots of Charley and me, smiling and in uniform. The text below them was unambiguous. The police wanted to question us urgently in relation to the Brian Minster case. It didn't specifically say we were dangerous, but it implied it.

'Now you're in trouble,' Rena said, strained.

The four of us stood in the kitchen, taking it in. The people in the adjacent homes were Rena's friends and neighbours, but that wouldn't stop them handing us over, not if they thought us a threat.

'I'm going into the village,' I said, 'to pick up some supplies. We need to move on.'

I opened the caravan door and walked outside, a slight tremor in my legs. I had no idea what I was doing, but we would need things – maybe some tins of food, a torch, rope, anything that might be used by people on the run.

I made it out of the field and started along the lane towards the village. It was a thirty-minute walk if I kept a steady pace. But, halfway there, I saw two police cars winding their way down the road ahead. Their blue lights were flashing, but their sirens were silent. For a few seconds, I couldn't move. This was the moment Dad had warned us about, the moment we'd been dreading; they were coming to get us.

The cars were far away enough for me not to have been seen. My sister was even further away at Rena's. If we ran, if we just ran fast enough, we might be able to evade them. I turned towards the caravan park and bolted. I ran back to Charley and Flint as though my life depended on it. Our bodies held a secret not even we knew. *No one must figure it out.*

Chapter 8

'What did your father do to you?' Gil repeats his question.

In the silence that follows, I feel I'm being strangled; I can hardly breathe. We feared the security services, we knew they'd ask that question, but we never imagined this.

'Please answer.' Gil's eyes lock on mine.

'Nothing,' I mutter. 'He didn't do anything to us.'

'Charley?' He turns to her, as though he hasn't heard me.

She shakes her head, no.

'Okay,' he says slowly, 'let me be clear. We can either have this conversation in a pleasant, open and honest way, or things will get difficult. I don't want anyone to get hurt, and I'm sure you don't either.'

We're silent, his threat ringing in our ears.

'I'm going to ask you for the final time,' he says matter-of-factly. 'What did your father do to you? Telling me he did nothing won't suffice.'

How can we possibly answer? I feel sick.

'We don't know,' Charley whispers, barely audible.

Gil stares at her a long moment.

'He didn't tell us,' she says. 'He didn't give us any details.'

'Well,' Gil says. 'Perhaps we can discuss this after all. Please, continue.'

'We don't know,' Charley repeats, louder, 'because…Dad…he left us a letter. He told us that he'd altered our genes, but he didn't tell us what he'd done to us.'

Gil's eyes don't move from her. I can't believe the risk she's taking, but then we've only got the truth.

'He didn't write it down, he didn't say,' she continues, upset. 'We don't know.'

Gil pauses, his face still. 'You almost sound convincing,' he says, 'but I'm afraid I don't believe you.'

The three guards surrounding us draw a little closer. The danger we're in is palpable.

'They don't know,' Flint blurts out aggressively. 'My uncle left them a shit letter. I got to read it too. It gave nothing away. It told them they'd been messed with, it didn't say how, and that was a shit thing for him to do.' He pauses but not for long. 'You can't ask people to tell you something they don't know!'

There is another silence. I feel a strange, temporary relief. Flint was brilliant. I couldn't have said it better myself, if I'd had the guts to speak.

Gil smiles at Flint but not in a mean way. 'I admire your desire to protect your cousins, and I like your energy, Flint, we can use that, but Charley and Dominic *do* know.'

'We don't,' I half shout. I need to speak up before something really awful happens. 'We've wanted to find you…*I've* wanted to find you,' I stress, 'because we thought *you* knew what he'd done to us.'

Gil looks surprised; he wasn't expecting that. 'Why would I know? What would make you think that?'

I almost say it: Kingfisher. Dad's code word. I thought I'd worked it out. I thought it led to Gil.

'Don't mention Kingfisher,' Charley screams into my head. *'It's not Gil. It was never Gil.'*

I flounder, struggling with what to say. 'H-he…' I stutter, 'he told you other secrets, we thought he'd have told you that too.' I have no idea what I sound like, if that's convincing.

Gil considers my words. 'There's a logic to that, but no, he never revealed any such thing.'

'So *you* don't know and *we* don't know,' I emphasise.

'I believe you do, Dominic,' he says quietly, and the look in his eyes is unrelenting.

We are in such trouble. Gil gets up and starts to move around the kitchen. He opens some of the drawers, pulls out a few knives, a pair of scissors and some wire cord. He looks around then walks over to the sink. It's a large, deep, ceramic sink. It belongs in a barn, it's so cracked and dirty; we tried cleaning it but didn't succeed. He puts in the plug and turns on the cold tap. Water splashes down. He leaves it to fill and checks the knives with the tips of his fingers, judging how sharp they are. An alarm bell starts ringing in my head. It just gets louder.

Flint turns to me; his face is anxious but his eyes instruct me to stay cool. Gil is winding us up. He's making out he's preparing to cut us, or hurt us, but it's a bluff. He'd never do that, not after all my father's done for him. I nod to Flint. I don't want fear to get the better of me, but beneath the table my legs are shaking involuntarily.

At last, the sink is full. Gil puts two knives he considers sharp enough on the table. He walks to the biggest guard in the room and whispers something in his ear. I fear this isn't a bluff; it's all too real. Then he stands before us. 'Now, how am I going to do this?' He queries, businesslike. His eyes flicker between us then stop on Charley. Of course, easy choice, go for the girl. My heart is racing.

'You can hurt me all you like,' Charley says, abnormally calm, 'but there is nothing I can tell you.' My sister's bravery is shocking and true. It seems to throw Gil. He turns his eyes slowly to Flint, whose face is blank, unperturbed; he's not going to let Gil get to him. Gil stands back a moment, thinking.

He moves quickly towards me. I feel his hand pull hard on my hair and then he's dragging me across the kitchen. I half stumble, moaning, shocked; he's pulling me by my hair. He thrusts me towards the sink. I see the water coming towards me, feel his arms pushing down on my head. My face is forced under. Another guard grabs my arms and holds them behind my back. I'm submerged, trapped. I took no deep breath in preparation. I realise what's happening too late.

I thrash out, desperate to get my face above the surface. I can't breathe. But Gil's hands are pushing down on me, and those constraining my arms are too powerful to throw. I can't escape their strength. But I need to get air. My body writhes, struggling against them. I'm running out of breath. Then Gil pulls my hair, drawing me out of the water. I'm gasping.

Charley's voice fills the room. 'Leave my brother alone. What are you doing to him? Stop!'

'I don't know what he did to us,' I cry out. 'I don't know, Gil.'

I hear Flint. 'Fuck you! Leave him alone.' There's a scuffle, someone is struck, and then he crumples back, moaning.

'Not good enough.' Gil shakes his head then pushes me down again.

I try to resist, but only manage a quick gulp of air before my face is underwater. I'm desperate; I fight furiously, but they just hold me tighter. The seconds extend, filled with horror. I don't have an answer. I don't know what my father did to us. He left only one word: Kingfisher. I thought I'd figured it out, but I was wrong. Everything is too late, and now I'm going to die.

CHAPTER 9

Four months earlier

Kingfisher. I became obsessed with that word – Dad's final clue. The search for its meaning started at Rena's. The weeks we spent with her were difficult. The days were long and listless, and my mood sank. When we'd lived with Dad, I'd always had some tune or line of music in my head but, at Rena's, the music stopped inside. Dad's letter silenced it. And any questions we had about him were impossible to pursue. We couldn't trawl the internet for fear of being traced, and Rena limited what we read, insisting it was lies and could only upset us.

But what Dad had done, and where he was now, preoccupied our minds. Charley tossed and turned in bed at night. Sometimes I'd hear her murmur in the dark, and I'd hug her tight for comfort. A few times I cried silently, frustrated and angry, but I wasn't sure if she knew. Dad left us his terrible truth but also a clue. I started to believe it might make sense of everything; it offered us help, if only we could figure it out.

'Rena,' I began, one afternoon when Rena sat in the kitchen with us. 'Dad sent us here because he trusted you. Does…' I paused, I needed to be careful. 'Does Kingfisher mean anything to you?' I'd said the word out loud.

'Kingfisher?' she queried, surprised. She shifted the mug in her hand. 'It's a bird, I know that.'

'But if you think of Dad,' I continued slowly, 'and then the word Kingfisher, does it mean anything to you?'

There was a pause, a space in which I sensed Rena withholding something.

'Does it?' I coaxed gently.

'It…makes me think of something that happened in our childhood,' Rena said quietly.

Charley and I both looked at her.

'I've…' She paused. 'For some reason it's always stayed with me.'

'Yes?' Charley encouraged her. Perhaps it had stayed in my father's memory too?

Rena spoke carefully. 'When I was about seven, and your father ten or eleven, we all went to this cottage in the country for the summer. I loved it there, running around in the fields, half naked and free, although Brian…well, he moaned he was bored. But one afternoon, I went and sat down by the river. I kept watching the water run over the stones and the roots of a tree there. And they looked like jewels, those stones, I remember them all bright and glistening. Then all of a sudden, out of nowhere, this amazing blue colour moved across the water, dived down, and then came up again. I had never seen anything like it, not that beautiful, or a colour so bright. And just as quickly as it was there, it was gone. I was so excited, I charged back to the cottage.

'"I've seen a blue spirit," I shouted, because that was the only way I could describe it, "down by the river, I've seen a blue spirit."

'"Have you?" my mother replied, and I explained what I saw. Brian was standing near her.

'"That's not a blue spirit," he said. "There's no such thing as blue spirits. You saw a kingfisher." Then he went and got his bird book to prove he was right. He always had to be right.

'"That's not what I saw," I told him, after he showed me the picture. "It wasn't a kingfisher, it was a blue spirit." I wouldn't budge any more than he would.

'So, of course, we had this big argument. Dad got so sick of our voices he sent us both outside, and we couldn't go back 'til supper. We spent the longest afternoon together sitting by that river. Brian wouldn't look at me, and he wouldn't speak to me. He just wanted to prove he knew best, and it was a kingfisher I'd seen. But it never showed itself again.'

'And that's it?' I said, unable to disguise my disappointment. I didn't know what I'd been expecting to hear, but it wasn't that. It didn't seem relevant. How could it be?

'I told you it wasn't much,' she said matter-of-factly. 'Although…it was probably the moment after which your dad and I started to drift apart. We'd been close, but that ended. Our lives took very different paths.' She paused. 'He never stopped thinking he knew best…not until…maybe, now.' Her voice trailed off. She shook her head. 'Poor Brian.'

I was upset; it was a useless memory. I needed more.

'*She doesn't know, Dom.*' Charley spoke into my thoughts. '*Leave it.*'

I didn't speak of Kingfisher again until the day the police came for us. I watched their vehicles winding down the road, blue lights flashing but sirens silent. I bolted back to Rena's. Charley and I packed quickly; we had to run. And then Flint made his decision. He'd join us. 'You'll never make it on your own,' he said without hesitation.

Flint hugged Rena tight. She kissed him hard on the forehead, and promised Charley that she would look after the kitten. Then the three of us charged out of the caravan, disappearing into the woodland beyond the campsite. We scattered among the trees and crouched down low. We never learnt what Rena told them, but the police didn't find us. We stayed still and silent for hours. Only after the sun had set, and the woodland was cloaked in darkness, did we come together again. I was cold and shivering.

'I thought they'd get us,' I confessed.

Flint shook his head. 'No chance. Rena would've sent them in the wrong direction.'

'But now what do we do?' Charley's teeth chattered.

'We keep low for the night,' Flint said. 'In the morning, I've an idea of where we can go.'

We huddled together; Charley was the first to fall asleep. I knew I wouldn't, keeping guard. I sensed Flint was equally alert.

'There's something you should know,' I whispered to him, 'now you're with us. I…I don't want there to be any secrets between us.' I paused. I felt him listening through the dark. Maybe I was taking a risk, but I had to say it. I trusted Flint. 'My father left us a code word: Kingfisher. We've no idea what he was trying to tell us, or what it means we should do, but I want you to know.'

'Cool,' he replied. 'I'm glad you told me.'

'Do you know what it might mean?' It was a long shot, but I asked anyway.

'Kingfisher? No idea. Although I guess he wasn't talking about the bird.'

'No,' I said with assurance. 'He's alluding to something or someone or…' I shrugged.

Flint was quiet, thinking. He shifted where he sat. 'I once had this teacher,' he said slowly, 'when Rena sent me to that church school in the village. His name was Mr Jenson, and he used to call Jesus the King Fisher.'

'The King Fisher?' I repeated, curious. I'd not heard that before.

'Yeah, 'cause in the Bible, Jesus's disciples, the guys who took his message out to people, they were called the fishers of men…the fishers of men's souls.' He paused. 'I don't know why, but I liked that phrase, guess it's why I remember it. Anyway…Mr Jenson said that as Jesus was their leader, he was the King Fisher.'

I listened to Flint and felt the strangest sensation. I didn't know much about religion, but if Jesus had disciples, and my father was accused of being involved with the Disciples, perhaps Flint was saying something important? But I also knew the papers were full of lies, and Dad never mentioned the Disciples, not once, not even that night he confessed to me, so Kingfisher couldn't relate to them. And Dad hated religion, he was a staunch atheist; he'd never leave us a clue that related to the Bible.

'Other than that,' Flint's voice interrupted my thoughts, 'I can't help you.'

'Dad despised religion,' I said, angry, because I was no closer to an answer. 'We never went to Sunday school or anything like that.' I was still angry. 'People do all sorts of terrible things in the name of religion.' Dad would say something similar.

'People also do terrible things in the name of science,' Flint said matter-of-factly.

I felt my throat tighten. 'Are you saying my father's a bad man?' I challenged, upset. The conversation wasn't going as I wanted.

'No, Dom,' he said gently. 'But he has done some bad things. What he did to you, that wasn't right.'

'He helped support you,' I reminded him. Flint didn't have a right to talk about my dad like that, only Charley and I did. 'Financially, he helped your mum out, and *you.*'

Flint paused before replying. I was really upset.

'Mum was in a lot of difficulty,' he said slowly, 'after Frank died. And…I know it took a lot for her to contact your dad. It wasn't easy…you who think you know everything. And…after she saw him, she never spoke about what happened.' He paused. I could hear him breathing hard. 'The only thing she ever said was that, despite everything, her brother could also be kind.'

'Kind?'

Flint nodded.

I closed my eyes. I didn't want to be this angry. 'Kind,' I said again. Why did everything feel so hard? 'I'm sorry,' I whispered. 'Sometimes I get so sick of things and the way nothing makes sense.'

'I guess.'

'I miss him,' I admitted, although I still couldn't look at Flint.

'Yeah, you do.'

'And…I have to find out what Kingfisher is.' I raised my eyes.

'You will, Dom. You will.'

The next day, Flint took us to the edge of the woodland. We all stared at a large mansion house behind a tall wall. It was isolated and looked uninhabited. There was nothing and no one around. Flint suggested we break in.

'No way,' I said, shaking my head. 'This is insane.' I didn't doubt my cousin indulged in the occasional illegal activity, but what he was suggesting was on a scale I hadn't anticipated.

'I've had my eye on this place for ages.' He smiled at me. 'Some rich guy built it, hardly ever uses it, and I say leaving a house like that unoccupied is a crime.' There was a hungry edge to his voice. 'Last year, he had some big summer party. Since then – nothing.'

'Flint, it's alarmed,' I said, anxious. 'That wired box on the front wall, JDL Securities, that's what keeps people out and brings the police in.'

Flint chuckled. 'Yeah, Dom, except a few days ago the red light at the top that shows it's rigged went out.' His eyes were bright. 'It ain't working anymore.'

The mansion was the antithesis of Rena's home. I wondered how long he'd been watching the place; it sounded like he was intending something.

'It's not right and it's too risky,' I said weakly.

Charley spoke up. 'Maybe we could just have a little look. In a way, given the housing crisis and how many people need a home, it really is a crime to leave a house like that unoccupied.'

I shook my head. What was happening to us? My sister didn't say things like that. We were justifying a criminal act. But, in the end, I helped Flint scale the wall. Whoever built the place wanted it to be private, and that worked in our favour. Flint smashed a small window at the back and broke in through the kitchen. I held my breath, waiting on the alarm shrieking, but there was only silence. Flint had been right.

The house was incredible: ultra-modern, minimalist in style, spotlessly clean. It oozed wealth from the massive kitchen to the wide staircase between the floors. We made our way through the rooms. They were luxurious. The beds were all made up, with extra cushions and plush covers, waiting on some future guests. Flint threw himself across one of them.

'Oh, yeah,' he said with satisfaction.

My sister went into one of the bathrooms and I heard running water. 'Oh, my God,' she exclaimed. 'This place is great.'

But the thing that mattered most to me was the computer in the study. I switched it on. It worked. The Wi-Fi connected. At last, away from Rena's constraints, and on an anonymous computer, I could find out what had happened to my father.

CHAPTER 10

There was a mass of information about Dad on the internet: newspaper articles, government statements, even a police blog. I lost myself in it for hours. Elsewhere in the house, I could hear Charley and Flint laughing. I left them to it; I had to digest what I was reading. But the more I read, the more it disturbed me. The eco-terrorist group, the Disciples, were mentioned again and again. Not a single report doubted my father's involvement with them. According to the police, references were found in Dad's emails to biblical quotes, and that was the coded way in which he communicated with them. The correspondence supposedly went back some time. But I knew my father: he'd only become political recently, and he hated religion. He was being set up. I despaired; he wouldn't get a fair trial.

I was about to switch it all off when my eyes stopped on a photo of Gil Zimmerman, the Disciples' leader. It was a family shot taken three years before. An older man and woman smiled at the camera while their son stood between them. Gil was ten years older than me. Dark hair framed his face, and his brown eyes seemed to look beyond the picture. According to what I was reading, after that photo was taken, he disappeared and the Disciples were born. The security services interrogated his parents, but they swore they knew nothing.

The Disciples' online propaganda didn't reveal individual members or claim Gil as their leader, but the police knew he was their key man. Grainy footage existed of the Disciples breaking into Enrosphere's refining plant, and Gil was there. I watched him turning his face from the camera and holding up two fingers in the victory sign. It was an act of defiance, taunting the police; he wasn't afraid.

Deputy Commissioner Alexandra Bray was quoted saying, 'We cannot stress how dangerous we consider this individual. His capacity to influence and recruit the young should not be underestimated.'

My eyes flipped between the family shot and the footage of his hand in the victory sign. A shiver ran down my spine. Somehow, he seemed familiar, as if I knew him. But how could that be possible? He was the leader of a terrorist group.

My sister's voice suddenly interrupted. 'Hey, Dom.' She stood in the doorway. 'You've got to see what we've found.'

I turned off the computer.

'Isn't this great?' Flint said. 'They were planning another party.'

We were in the basement. They had found a stash of champagne.

'I've never seen so much,' I said, amazed. There was more booze there than in an off-licence.

We cracked open a bottle. There was party food too: nuts, crisps, nibbling snacks. Most were past their use-by date, but we didn't care and they tasted good.

'I like this place.' My sister smiled.

'Yeah,' I agreed, although I knew we couldn't get used to it.

'What d'you find out?' Flint asked, opening a second bottle.

Champagne's strong stuff. I knew I was getting drunk and was unsure if I wanted to discuss it.

'Everything I've read's upsetting, insisting Dad's been involved with the Disciples.' It was a blunt statement.

'It's lies,' Charley said. 'You know that.'

'I know.' I sighed. 'But…what gets me most is nobody's writing anything else. They're all taking it as true. He'll…he'll get no justice.'

'Course not,' Flint said. 'It's what the authorities want people to think. They're wrecking it for him before he gets to trial.'

I looked at Flint and nodded, but then I saw Gil's image in my mind. I shivered again.

'The thing is…' I continued, 'it makes me feel confused, because I…' I stopped a moment. 'A part of me's afraid that maybe it *is* true.' I swallowed hard.

'Dom,' Charley said, 'what are you saying? That Dad hid even more from us than he revealed in that letter?'

I paused before responding, aware my head felt fuzzy. 'Maybe. I think that's possible.'

'Bollocks,' Flint retorted. 'You've been reading all their shit and letting it affect you. That's what they want, Dom. Everybody's gotta hate the traitor, Brian Minster.' His expression told me I should know better. 'They're messing with your head.'

'This whole thing, from the moment Dad started to tell me about it, has been messing with my head!' I shouted. 'I'm upset, okay? I don't know what's going on. And I'm afraid that maybe what I'm reading is true.'

Flint's eyes held mine. He almost smiled. 'Then you better stop reading,' he said gently. 'Drink up and forget about it.'

Later, when my body was intoxicated and my mind empty of worries, we all crashed out on one of the king-size beds. I closed my eyes, giggling. The world was spinning, and then it was quiet. Sweet oblivion for a while.

I woke, disorientated. Where was I? An unfamiliar room. I vaguely remembered: we got drunk, we put on some music, we danced. Charley and Flint looked good together. I moved like a maniac. Then I remembered we were also on the run and we'd made a lot of noise. Oh, no, that wasn't good. Somebody could have heard us. We weren't safe. I turned on the bed. Charley and Flint were lying beside me. We were all fully clothed, sprawled out near each other. My body felt like lead, but I knew I should wake them. We weren't safe, only I realised I had no idea what we'd do next. I flopped back down.

If Dad were here now, he wouldn't be impressed with our behaviour. He could be strict. I imagined him telling me off; that was comforting. I missed the way the world felt ordered when he was around. Then my thoughts shifted to what I'd read. What had my father really been doing?

'I know you're not a bad man, Dad,' I whispered into the room. 'I just wish you were here to explain.'

I closed my eyes and imagined him as he'd been that night we spoke in the kitchen. I saw him clearly in the clothes he'd been wearing, and the beer he'd half drunk on the table.

'What *did* you do, Dad?' I asked him in my imagination. 'I need the truth.' I was carrying on the conversation, asking the questions I didn't know then. I waited on his reply.

'You're smart, Dominic. You can figure it out.' His voice was in my thoughts; everything about him felt real.

'No, Dad,' I replied. 'I'm struggling, I've been struggling with it all.'

'Try,' he said.

'Are you…are you involved with the Disciples? They're saying you are, that you have been for some time.'

There was a long pause between us. 'You know I can't answer that. I want to protect you, that's all that counts.'

I tried another question. 'They're saying you communicated in biblical quotes, but why would you do that? You're not religious, you hate religion.'

Again, there was a long pause before he answered. 'If I were to communicate in code, what better cover could I have than to use one nobody might associate me with?'

I swallowed hard. That *did* make sense in an espionage story kind of way. But there was one last question, maybe the most important of all.

'What or who is Kingfisher?'

He didn't reply. Instead, his image in my mind started to break up. I was no longer with him, no longer standing in the kitchen. I was lying on a bed in a stranger's house. I shouldn't be there. I realised I was crying. I felt unbearably sad.

Kingfisher. Why did he leave us that word? Rena had some childhood memory about a blue spirit and a bird book. It was no help at all. And Flint had a teacher who said Jesus was the King Fisher. That was no help either, unless…those press reports were true. If they were, Dad would have known we'd get to read about his use of biblical code. *We're not stupid, we might put two and two together.* So…if Jesus was the leader of his disciples and a King Fisher and Gil Zimmerman was leader of the Disciples then…

I froze. I felt very nauseous and not from the alcohol. My mind was frantic. Then a blue light streaked across the ceiling. It was from a passing car only it didn't seem to be moving on. Instead, the light kept whirring. Flint stirred beside me, his eyes opening. It was the blue light of a police car.

'Shit!' I sat up.

Flint was suddenly very alert. 'Oh, no.' He scrambled from the bed and crouched down low by the window. 'Police,' he whispered, 'but they're on the other side of the wall. They're looking at the house, but I don't reckon they can see us.'

'We've got to get out of here,' I said, jittery. I wished I hadn't drunk so much.

Charley woke up. 'What going on?'

'We've got to get out of here,' I repeated. 'The police are outside.'

'What?' She bolted upright.

'Calm down,' Flint hissed, indicating we keep low. 'They're driving off.' The blue light faded.

I saw the truth clearly, and it was terrible.

CHAPTER 11

We no longer felt safe. The police could return at any moment. We had to move on.

'The first thing we must do,' Flint said, pacing the room, 'is change your appearance. You can't walk around looking like those photos in the paper. And we need to change our names…and come up with a story.'

It sounded like he was planning a heist – like we were living out a movie. I needed to speak to them about Kingfisher, but it wasn't the moment.

Flint risked going out to pick up a few items, and when he returned he got to work on Charley's hair. He cut away her long locks.

'I once worked as a hairdresser's assistant,' he told her. 'I'm going for that elf look: short, feathery and cute.'

Silent tears tracked my sister's cheeks. She loved having long hair, but she wasn't going to argue with him. We had to do whatever it took to stay safe. She then went into the bathroom and dyed her hair black. I was going to try and grow a goatee beard, not that I had much facial hair.

We agreed on a story to explain our lives. We were no longer family, but friends who'd met at school. We took new names. I was Luke, Charley was Sophie, and Flint, Jake. Charley stood in front of the mirror, transfixed by her new image. 'Soph,' she said, unsure of herself.

'You look different, but good.' Flint smiled.

She caught his eyes. For a moment, I thought she might cry again. She didn't believe him.

'How many guys d'you kiss before?' he asked gently.

'None, and now my chances have zeroed.'

He shook his head kindly. 'I'm not so sure about that.' He moved to her and without warning placed the lightest kiss upon her lips. It wasn't really sexual, just tender. My sister didn't move, and I told myself it was a one-off. He was trying to cheer her up, but a small smile curled the edge of her lips.

I decided to speak. 'Listen, I've figured out Kingfisher.' I took a few deep breaths to keep myself calm. I was going to say things that would be hard to hear. 'It's Gil Zimmerman. The leader of the Disciples.'

Silence followed. Flint and Charley looked at me as though I'd lost the plot.

'I've tried to avoid believing it,' I continued quickly. 'I've wanted it to be different, but now I know what I read yesterday is true. Dad's involved with the Disciples.' I paused, gathering my thoughts. 'He communicated with them in biblical code, because it's the last thing you'd imagine him doing, and that's how he's communicated with us. Flint, in a way, got it.' I explained to Charley what he'd said.

All the time I was talking, Flint shook his head slowly. 'Dominic,' he said, once I'd finished, 'we don't have time for this. We've gotta get out of here.'

'This is key to what we do next,' I said firmly.

I turned to Charley; she looked pale. 'Dom, you don't really believe this, do you?'

I felt my lower lip tremble. 'Yes, I do. It makes sense. Dad loved us, Charley. He left us that word for a reason. He knew we'd be running once they got to Rena's. We'd have nowhere to hide.

Kingfisher can help.' I stopped, I was breathing quickly. My own words were scaring me.

'What are you saying?' Charley asked slowly. 'That you think Gil Zimmerman can help us?'

I nodded, yes. 'Maybe he knows what Dad did to us,' I whispered. 'Maybe he's the only help we have.'

'Bullshit,' Flint interrupted. 'No way. Your dad wrote you a letter, he told you to run, he never mentioned the Disciples. You can't believe this.'

'He wrote us a letter that left out as much as it left in. And I know I'm right, Flint, because I know my father.'

Flint's animosity to what I was saying was clear, but Charley was unsure. I focused on my sister.

'There's something about Gil Zimmerman,' I told her, 'that's familiar. That makes me think I've seen him before. I know that doesn't make sense, but I need you to trust me on this.' Then I spoke directly into her head. '*He didn't tell us about the Disciples because it would have been too dangerous.*' There were things between Charley and I that Flint could never understand. '*He wanted to protect us.*'

'If you're right,' Charley said carefully, 'what does that mean we should do?'

'We need to find him.' My words hung in the air.

'How d'you think you're going to do that?' Flint asked, his voice cold.

'I don't know,' I answered honestly. 'But I'll think of something.' I really had no idea, but I hated his attitude. 'Considering you know how to break into mansions, and shoplift, and no doubt engage in other criminal activities, maybe you know?' I was pushing him. Everything felt on edge.

Flint's eyes narrowed on me; I think he wanted to hit me. 'Oh yeah,' he said. I could feel his anger rising. 'I can tell you what to do.

They'll be hard to find, but what you do is start asking questions in the kind of places where they might have contacts. That will arouse their suspicion, and then *they'll find you,*' he stressed, 'but only if the police haven't got you and locked you up already. Either way, you'll have had it.'

'I get that it's risky,' I said, as though what he'd suggested was possible.

'Risky? No, Dom.' He shook his head. 'It ain't risky, it's reckless. I've done some dangerous things in my time, but I won't stick around to see this.'

There was a strained silence.

'I understand,' I said slowly. 'You've helped us a lot, Flint, and your position's clear. Charley and I will take it from here.'

He flew at me, his hands hard against my chest. The force pushed me back into the wall. I was winded.

'I've not come all this way to watch you commit suicide.' He was close to tears. 'You have no idea. And what about what Charley wants?'

'Charley and I know how important Kingfisher is and we'll pursue it together,' I said with as much authority as I could. Flint and I were about to strike each other.

'Stop it!' Charley shouted. 'Both of you. Stop it! And don't talk about me as though I'm not standing here perfectly capable of speaking for myself.' She was shaking with emotion. 'I can't bear you fighting. I don't want us to fight.'

Flint and I turned to her, stunned.

'I don't know what we should do,' she continued, 'but I want us to do whatever it is together.' She looked bewildered. 'The police were here earlier, they'll probably be back. We can't afford to fight like this. We have to stick together.'

I realised I was trembling. Flint was too. We had to calm down.

'I'm…I'm with you, not against you,' Flint said after a pause. 'And…you're in danger, we can't mess up. I know it hurts,' he turned to Charley, 'but your dad betrayed you. He did things to you he never should've. So…even if Dom's got it right about Kingfisher, you can't follow it. The Disciples are dangerous people,' he focused on me, 'and that guy Gil Zimmerman, he's got his own agenda. Look where your dad is now – I can't see them helping him. You go to the Disciples, Dom, and you might as well go to the police, 'cause they're as bad as each other.'

I wasn't going to fight Flint, but I also had something to say. 'The thing is, Flint, you don't have a father, so you don't understand. Dad loved us. He wants us to find Gil because he can help. He wouldn't put us in more danger.'

Our eyes met.

He shook his head again, gently. 'You may have a father, Dom, but he's done things to you that you wouldn't have believed possible two or three months ago. So how come you're so sure you know him and he's not wrong now?'

I couldn't answer that. I couldn't find the words to explain how I felt inside. My breath was heavy in my chest.

'What d'you think?' Flint turned to Charley. Her eyes flitted between the two of us.

'I don't know,' she said, anxious. 'I know Dad loved us…and I understand what you're saying, Dom.' She paused. 'But…the thought of trying to contact terrorists.' Her eyes met mine. 'I can't do it,' she whispered. 'It's too scary. They're too dangerous and…what if you're wrong, Dom? What if Dad's Kingfisher *isn't* Gil Zimmerman?'

I closed my eyes against the tears I could feel welling up. I couldn't believe I was going to cry; Charley was siding with Flint. She'd never done anything like that before, but his words held more sway than mine. I was alone.

'I'm sorry, Dom,' she said gently. '*I love you,*' she continued into my head. '*I don't think you're right on this, but I still love you.*'

A few hot tears escaped my closed eyelids. I couldn't speak or look at them. I felt too hurt. I knew we were ignoring Dad's help; we were letting him down, but they couldn't see it. Flint was silent, and then I felt his hand touch my shoulder.

'You okay?' he asked softly.

It took me a while before I could speak. 'So what do we do then?' I opened my eyes.

'I reckon we've two choices,' Flint said slowly. 'One, we head for London. It's a large, anonymous city, an easy place to hide out in. We could find a squat or somewhere like that and disappear, for all they know.'

'No,' I responded quickly. 'I don't want to go back to the city I love, not to live a different life to the one we had with Dad.'

'Me neither,' Charley agreed.

Flint hesitated. 'What about Manchester then – or Birmingham?'

'I hate the idea,' I said. Charley shook her head, no, too.

'Then option two is we disappear into the countryside,' Flint said. 'Not round here, but head north. Slip into Scotland and keep going up the map. From what I've seen, you get to those northern, highland areas, and you're in isolated, rural land. The people are independent minded. I reckon we could be safe there.'

Neither Charley nor I responded. It went beyond anything we'd considered.

'We'll stand out, Flint,' I finally said. 'It's been bad enough in this village.'

'I don't think so,' Flint replied. 'It's holiday season now. There'll be other English people up there, even some with dark skin like me. And Mum knew this guy called Joey – he lived near her and then he went up to the Highlands. He wrote to her and said it was the best thing he'd ever done. It was beautiful and peaceful, and nobody knew who he was, which was good considering he was an ex-con trying to start again.'

Still, Charley and I were quiet.

'There aren't many options,' Flint pointed out.

'Would you like to go to Scotland?' Charley asked him.

'I'll go wherever you two want,' he replied. 'But yeah, I'd like to go to Scotland. It'd be something new.'

'Do you *really* think we'll be safe?' I asked.

'As safe as we can be.'

'Then let's go,' my sister said, trying to smile.

I nodded in agreement; there wasn't much choice. I felt hollow inside.

We left later that day. We thought Scotland would be safe.

CHAPTER 12

Gil holds my head underwater. The air in my lungs is ebbing away. I'm going to have to breathe and when I do, I'll drown. I strain to stay in control, my lungs aching. But I'm not going to be able to hold out. They're killing me.

My body writhes and then Gil pulls me up again. I cough, splutter and gasp as I reach the air. I hear my sister screaming, begging them to stop; there's nothing we can tell them. But I'm finding it hard to concentrate. I'm gulping down air, yet I'm light-headed.

'Do you want to die?' Gil's voice is ferocious in my ear.

'No.' I struggle to speak.

'Are you going to tell me what I need to know?' His hand pulls hard on my hair.

'If I could, I would.'

'The next time your head goes under, I'm not bringing it up until we can bury you. So think…remember…very carefully. What did your father do to you?'

'Gil,' I plead. 'I promise you, I'm telling the truth. I don't know. He didn't tell us.'

His hand tightens on me. He's preparing to push me under again.

These are my final moments. 'I don't know!' I scream.

Gil jerks my head back. His breath is on my face. 'I hoped you'd tell the truth. But now, it's got to end like this.'

I know I'm going to die. 'Gil, please, don't do this to me.' I sound animal; I've never heard myself sound like that.

He shakes his head.

'I'm begging you. Don't do this to me!'

He pushes me down again. The water is coming towards me. The world slows. Charley is shrieking in the background. I know however much I struggle, I can't get free. My face is breaking through the water's surface.

'*I love you, Dom,*' Charley says into my head. They're the last words I'll hear.

'*I love you too, Charley.*' Then my head is submerged.

I use every ounce of my strength to thrash against them, yet their arms are like vices holding me. Gil pushes my forehead hard against the bottom of the sink; I'm not sure if he'll break my neck before he drowns me. Images flash through my mind: Charley, Flint, Mary. I've only lived sixteen years, yet at least I've known love. I see Dad. I don't know where he is now, but maybe he's dead too? Maybe I'll finally meet him again? I don't know if drowning hurts, but it should be quick. I just want it to be over quick.

Gil's strength is unrelenting; he doesn't give an inch. He's not going to bring my head up. My lungs are desperate for air, the pressure inside them intense. It won't be a voluntary action, breathing, because of course it will kill me. But my lungs don't know that, they just want to breathe. This is it. The end. I'm empty of air.

My mouth opens. I breathe. I wait for the pain of water filling my lungs and then sinking into unconsciousness. It doesn't happen. I breathe in. I breathe out. A few bubbles release from my mouth and go up to the water's surface. I breathe in and out again. My head is submerged. I should be drowning; I should be dead, but I'm not. I'm breathing underwater. I watch as with each breath I take bubbles rise to the surface. My thoughts still. I'm transfixed by the bubbles rising from my mouth.

Gil raises my head slowly from the sink. I cough and splutter as I hit the air again, my lungs readjusting. The kitchen is silent. Nothing moves. Something has happened and it's to do with me.

'Good boy,' Gil says gently. 'I knew you'd do it in the end.'

My body starts shaking and then I'm sobbing. I don't know why. I thought I was dead. I'm still alive.

'Now we know,' he says.

What am I? Human beings don't breathe underwater, except I have. My legs start to buckle under me but Gil holds me up.

'It's over, Dominic,' he says calmly. 'That was cruel, I know, but it's over now.'

'I can't stop shaking.' My teeth chatter. He guides me slowly to a chair; I sit.

Charley's crying too; her voice hiccups. Flint's face is pale and blood streaks his forehead. Someone puts a blanket over my shoulders, but I can't get warm. The three guards move around us. Two of them disappear upstairs and then our rucksacks are in the kitchen, our things stuffed inside.

'We need to go,' Gil instructs. 'It's not safe here.'

The woman picks up our rucksacks and takes them outside. The other two men indicate that Flint and Charley should follow them.

'I can't move,' I say.

Gil yanks me up. 'Put your arm around my shoulder.'

Somehow, I stagger outside. He doesn't seem bothered by the weight of my body against him. There are two trucks. Gil orders Charley and Flint to go with the men in one. The woman will drive the two of us in the other.

'No,' I say. He's splitting us up. I can't be without Charley and

Flint. I don't know if I'll see them again. 'I've got to go with them.'

'I make the decisions,' Gil says firmly, 'and you will come with me.'

I start to struggle against him, but he holds me tighter. 'Stop it, Dominic. You really don't want to fight. We travel in two trucks, because it's safer. We're all going to the same destination, just by two different routes. You'll see them again soon.'

I look at him. His eyes tell me that now he's made that clear, he expects me to obey. I glance at Charley and Flint. They look stunned. None of us want any of this, but there isn't a choice. I move with Gil into the back of a truck. There are no windows, only tarpaulin hanging over a basic metal structure. We turn to shadow. At first I feel panic at the quiet and dark, but then relief. The other truck moves off first. We wait a while before driving away. I'm cold and weary. The rumble of the wheels on the road provides a lulling sensation. I rest my head back, exhausted.

'You should try and get some sleep,' Gil says quietly.

'Are we going far?'

'It'll be a while,' he says, which tells me nothing.

I close my eyes, but sleep won't come. I'm alone in a truck with a man who tried to kill me. I've never known such terror. No wonder I can't sleep.

'My f…fa…father,' I stutter. I want to tell Gil he'd hate him for what he did tonight. He'd never forgive him, but instead I end up crying again. At least this time it's silent and the truck is too dark for him to see me properly. He doesn't respond. I try to continue but can't.

Later, I hear him. 'We'll discuss your father another time.'

I have no idea what my father was doing with the Disciples; they're dangerous, violent people. And I feel wretched, knowing for sure he was involved with them. I can never pretend otherwise.

'I've done nothing wrong to you,' I whisper, distressed, 'but you would have killed me tonight.'

'No, Dominic,' Gil replies, unperturbed. 'I would never have killed you. I just needed you to believe I was capable of it.' There is a long pause between us. 'You may hate me tonight,' he says slowly, 'but that will change.'

A strange sound escapes my lips. No.

'Try and get some sleep,' he says softly.

I close my eyes and stifle a sob rising in my throat. I can feel his presence through the dark and silence. Even with my eyes shut, I still feel him there.

CHAPTER 13

'Dominic, wake up.'

Someone shakes my shoulder. I open my eyes. Where am I? I see Gil's face and remember.

'We're here.' He instructs me to get down.

I shift out of the back of the truck. We're parked outside a large, imposing manor house. Beyond it, I can see only darkness; it spreads out in every direction, over fields perhaps or hillside. The other truck arrives and Charley and Flint get down. It feels a long time since I saw them. We're tired and disorientated. A bandage has been applied to Flint's head where previously I'd seen blood.

Gil motions us towards the house. The door opens and a bearded man looks out. He registers our presence and grins. He holds the door back and we walk through. It's dark inside, but I sense people waiting there. The door is shut behind us and then the lights go on. My eyes scrunch up against the sudden brightness.

We are standing in a spacious open hallway. There are wood panels on the walls, a huge but empty fireplace, and an old-fashioned chandelier. At least fifteen people are staring at us: men and women dressed like the ones who've been holding us. Their clothes need a wash. They're in jeans or khaki trousers; some men have long hair and some women look like men. A lot have piercings and tattoos. There are a few moments' silence as they take us in.

'Well done, Gil,' the bearded man says. He moves forward to hug Gil; they embrace. Then a round of applause erupts in the hallway. Everyone's smiling. Gil raises an arm to quiet them.

'Okay, everybody,' he says clearly, 'as you can probably tell… we've had a bit of a rough night.'

A few people nod. I feel exposed; their eyes don't move from us. My hair is tangled and I smell the fear I experienced earlier as sweat in my clothes.

'So,' Gil continues, 'I think we should show our *guests* to their room.' He stresses the word 'guests'. Surely they know we're not there by choice? 'Let them get a good night's rest, and we can take things forward in the morning.'

There is a communal nod of assent.

'Chloe,' Gil says to a woman with shoulder-length red hair, 'take them as we agreed, up to the loft.'

Chloe steps forward and smiles at us. She has a gap between her two front teeth. I wonder how long they've planned this for. I shift my eyes momentarily to Gil, and he indicates we should follow her.

The house is enormous, spread out over three floors. There is a loft at the top where space has been cleared for us. Boxes have been pushed aside and a large rug thrown across the floorboards. There are three sleeping bags, some pillows and blankets. I'm relieved that at least we're all together. I couldn't be on my own tonight.

'The bathroom's on the next floor down,' Chloe says, sounding friendly. 'We keep it pretty relaxed here, so there are no locks on any of the doors. And with only three bathrooms, you can't hog the space.'

'What about having a shit?' Flint asks. I don't know if he's being serious or teasing.

'The same,' Chloe continues, smiling. 'There's no point getting hung up about natural smells, is there?' She shrugs.

None of us respond. It's clear there is nowhere we will be alone; we have no privacy. An awkward silence spreads between us.

'Anyway,' she says, 'you're probably tired. I'll leave you now unless there's anything you'd like to eat or drink?'

'No thanks,' Charley replies. Flint turns away; he's had enough. Chloe moves to leave.

'Whisky,' I say. 'I'd like some whisky.' I want to feel its hot, burning taste roll down my throat. I want it to help me stop feeling the way I do now.

'Whisky?' Chloe repeats.

I nod, yes. She disappears. I don't expect to get it, but I'm glad I said it. Maybe they'll get the message. The three of us stand there, silent, looking at each other. We're all too upset to speak. Then Charley rushes forward and embraces me. She hugs me tight, her nails digging into my shoulders.

'Dom.' She keeps saying my name over and again. *I thought they were going to kill you,* she whispers into my head. *I couldn't have borne it if they had.*

'Please don't make me cry again,' I mutter. 'I don't want to cry.'

'I hate them,' Flint says bitterly. 'It was so easy for them to hurt us.' He comes over and joins our hug. Charley's head is buried in my chest, but I meet Flint's eyes. 'They should never have done that,' he whispers. He shakes his head. I know he's angry, but he's also afraid.

'I've no idea what happens now,' I say. 'I don't know how we get away.'

None of us have the answer to that. Instead, we slowly release each other.

'I'm going to the bathroom.' Charley takes her toiletries out of her rucksack. 'I just hope it's empty.' She disappears.

Flint starts to lay out the sleeping bags. Charley returns and then he goes downstairs. I watch as they get into what will be our beds. But I'm not functioning well. I should be getting out of my clothes and under a blanket. I'm cold, but I'm not moving.

The door to the loft opens and Gil comes in. It's noticeable he didn't knock before entering. He glances at Charley and Flint then comes towards me.

'Here,' he says. 'Whisky.' He passes me the glass; he's poured a lot into it.

I take it and look into his eyes. He's quite calm. 'I'm only sixteen,' I tell him, breathing quickly, because I can't help being afraid. 'Too young, supposedly, for this.' I raise the glass.

'Indeed,' Gil acknowledges. 'But…I'm not one to condemn illegal acts.' He almost smiles. 'Hopefully that will help you sleep. We can talk in the morning.'

'I'm too young to die, too,' I blurt out. My hand shakes slightly.

Gil's expression is serious. 'Indeed,' he says again. Then after a pause, 'We won't let that happen.'

No, I think, not unless you're doing the killing.

Gil turns his gaze to Charley and Flint. 'Just so you're all aware: the landscape here is beautiful – you'll see it in the morning. We're isolated. There isn't another inhabited building for miles, and it's pitch black outside. We ensure our safety by always having two people on guard all night.'

His voice is pleasant and matter-of-fact, but we get what he's really saying. If we think we are going anywhere, if we have any thought of escape, we can forget it. He exits. I gulp back the whisky and get inside my sleeping bag. I pull it up and over my head.

They let us lie in. I wake the next morning with a sense of dread. The events of the night before swirl in my head. Chloe eventually returns and takes us down to a large dining area for breakfast. It's quickly clear that everywhere in the house is a communal space.

While we eat, some women and a few of the men come over to introduce themselves. Tom, in particular, holds a position of authority; he's Gil's second in command. His blond hair and beard contrast with Gil's dark features. They are all friendly to us, which is disturbing in its way; they act like we've chosen to be there.

'We're all brothers and sisters here,' Chloe says. She never seems to stop smiling. Is that her job – to somehow try and make us feel welcome? It won't work. We're not stupid.

'It's okay, thanks,' Charley replies politely. 'One brother is enough for me.'

Once we've eaten, Tom escorts us down a corridor to Gil's room. It's an impressive study, full of shelves with books and manuals. There is a table with a leather top and a mix of wooden chairs around it. Papers are scattered here and there. Gil stands at one of the large windows looking out at the rugged landscape, his back to us. The cloud is low in the sky, the light in the room suffused with a blue-grey tinge.

Tom indicates we should sit at the table. There is a long period of silence, a space in which I feel the tension rising inside me.

'Is this your base?' I ask, because the silence is too uncomfortable. 'Your headquarters?'

Gil turns to us. He doesn't reply immediately. He is one of the few men at the house who is clean-shaven, and his pale skin stands out against his dark hair. But it's his eyes that get me. They have a piercing quality as though he can see right through me. And suddenly something clicks; I realise why I felt I knew him. He looks like Jesus: the Jesus I've seen in paintings in museums, and in pictures in books, only without the beard. I'm shocked I didn't realise it before. He looks like Jesus and leads the Disciples. The fishers of men's souls.

'This house,' he says, 'is on the land of a wealthy and influential man. He has friends in parliament, and positions in some of the companies we're most determined to bring down.'

We are quiet. None of us imagines he wants us to speak.

'He's our inside man.' Gil half smiles. 'What better place could we operate from? Who is going to question or enter the private property of such an esteemed member of the establishment?' He moves to sit at the head of the table. 'I trust you slept well,' he enquires softly.

Still, none of us respond.

'Listen…' he continues in a confiding manner, 'yesterday was a difficult start. I would have liked it to have been easier, but things don't always work out as we want.'

I glance back at Tom standing in the doorway. He watches Gil intently. I wonder if they've planned this all; I think so.

'Your father,' Gil says, his eyes moving between Charley and me, 'was a brave and conscientious man, prepared to take the ultimate risk for his convictions. I…I hope we can all see him again someday.'

'You don't even know where he is,' I retort.

'He's in one of three possible locations,' Gil assures me.

'Is he still alive?'

'Everyone interrogated has their breaking point. He's still speaking to them, which means he's still alive. They won't kill him.'

'Breaking point?' Charley whispers, her face pale. I feel sick.

'I'm afraid so. I tell the truth,' Gil informs us bluntly. 'If you ask me a question, I'll give you the answer, but it may not be easy to hear.'

'Are you going to let us go?' Flint asks boldly. I love my cousin.

Gil sits back in his chair. 'I'd like to make a proposal,' he says slowly. 'That you join us, the Disciples. I'll tell you why.'

His face is serious. I'm breathing too quickly. I don't want to hear what he says next.

CHAPTER 14

'When I look at you,' Gil says softly, 'I see three bright, intelligent people. Young people with enormous potential, and yet the world we live in won't respect that.' He pauses a moment. 'Do you know who told us where you were?'

We're silent. He's going to reveal who betrayed us.

'Gregory.'

I feel my face twitch, the tension tight. Gregory, Mary's father. It was his cottage we were staying in.

'Do you know why?' Gil continues.

'He didn't want me sleeping with his daughter,' I say loudly. I'm almost shaking. I can't find the words to express how upset I feel. Sweet, kind Mary, trapped by her father. He hated me. He betrayed us all.

'Sleeping with his daughter?' Gil responds, bemused. 'What are you on about?'

A strange half laugh escapes my lips. Everything is a jumble. I've said too much; it's not what Gil means. He waits a moment until I'm still.

'Gregory knew other local people had recognised you,' he continues, ignoring my outburst. 'One, in particular, had informed the police. He understood the danger you were in. He'd considered contacting us before, and finally found the courage to do so.'

All along, Gregory had his own agenda. Poor Mary, I'll probably never see her again.

'If MI5 had got to you first, where do you think you would have been last night?' Gil's question hangs in the air. 'Would they have let you stay together, or even have allowed you to sleep? What might they have done to you by now?' He raises his eyebrows, questioning us. 'And all we've shown you here is respect and friendship.'

'What?' I reply, shocked. 'You nearly killed me. Had I not been able to breathe underwater, you would have killed me.'

Gil shakes his head. 'I would never have let you die, Dominic, but you do need to understand how serious this is. There's a war going on and you're a part of it now. Your father understood that. The forces that prop up capitalism, that keep the rich and corrupt in power, come down hard, relentlessly, on people like you, me and your father.' His eyes are bright; they seem to spark with energy. 'Where would you be if the police had got you?'

We're silent.

Then Charley speaks. 'We won't join you. We don't know what the police would've done to us. Maybe terrible things. But you're terrorists. You plant bombs, you blow things up, and you hurt people. You *hurt* my brother,' she stresses. 'We won't join you.'

Gil is still, thinking. He stays calm, but that doesn't make me feel any safer.

'What happened to your brother last night will never happen again,' he says, focusing on Charley. 'Dominic will be safe here, as will you and Flint. We can protect you from the police and MI5. They'll never get you while you're with us. We'll provide for all your everyday needs: food, clothing, shelter. And in return…for that safety and security…all we ask for is a little loyalty. You will never be asked to hurt anyone,' he states plainly. 'I would send you out on only a few, very select operations. And even then only one, at the maximum two of you, would go out at the same time. Otherwise, you'll be safe here.' He pauses. 'Is that really so difficult?'

I realise what I knew from the start of this conversation. The Disciples are never going to let us go.

'What if it is?' Flint asks. 'What if we refuse, if we cause trouble, if we're happier to take our chances on our own?' He can barely control his defiance.

'You don't want to go there,' Gil says gently.

'Yes, I do,' Flint insists. 'You're a fucking terrorist. You don't ask nicely. You never do that. What are you going to do if we refuse?' His rage bristles.

'We'll hurt you so badly, Flint,' Gil whispers, 'your cousins will be begging me to stop. They'll offer anything to stop seeing you in the kind of pain we can inflict.'

Something about the brutality of Gil's words, and the softness of his voice, is so menacing I feel light-headed. Flint grows very still. We're in a nightmare, one we can't wake up from.

'Now,' Gil continues, 'I suggest you go back up to the loft. Consider your situation, and I'll see you again in an hour.'

Although we're dismissed, none of us can move, frozen by his threat. Tom eventually pulls Charley's chair back, forcing her to stand. She walks out the room and Flint follows. I rise to leave.

'Dominic.' Gil stops me. He walks over. He's uncomfortably close. 'Don't mistake me for your enemy,' he says slowly. 'Your enemy is out there, and you may not recognise it yet, but I'm your friend.'

My mouth feels parched, dry. 'No friend would threaten Flint like you just have.'

He leans over until I can feel his breath on my skin. 'I'm not going to hurt Flint,' he whispers in my ear, 'but I'm not going to let the other side get you either. I promised your father I'd protect you. He loved you and knew how special you are.'

I close my eyes. Gil makes my head spin. How can he talk about my father like that? I open my eyes again and look into his face. Did he meet Dad? Did they really discuss such things?

'I loved my father,' I tell him, 'but I've no idea who he is anymore.'

'He's a Disciple,' Gil says firmly. 'Understand that, and you know him again.'

I'm barely breathing. I'm afraid and I'm upset. I leave his room and run quickly up the stairs. There's a tingling sensation in my hands and feet. Charley and Flint turn to me as I close the loft door.

'What else did he have to say?' Charley's voice bites. She's distraught.

'He's not going to hurt Flint. I think he meant it, but…he's not going to let us go either. He won't let the other side get us.'

Flint shakes his head slowly – he's almost in tears. 'That man is wicked. I swear I'd kill him if I could.'

'Flint, stop.' I know this won't help. 'We've got to accept…' I pause. I try again. 'We're…we're go…going to have to join the Disciples.'

'No!' my sister screams. 'We are not joining the Disciples.'

'We don't have a choice,' I tell her.

'We will not give in to threats.' Charley's charged with rage. 'If he goes near Flint, he'll have to take me on first.'

'Charley,' I say loudly. She needs to listen. 'He's not going to hurt Flint, but we still don't have a choice. We have nowhere to go, there is nowhere to hide.' Then before either she or Flint can protest, I continue. 'Dad was involved with Gil. He was a Disciple. We can't escape that either.'

My sister is silent; she finally understands. I watch as tears start to slide down her cheeks.

'I hate the truth,' I whisper. 'It's stabbing my heart, because I love Dad so much. But…now…' I take a deep breath. 'I can see that Gil *is* Kingfisher, so there's nowhere else to go. We have to face that fact.'

The tears keep running down my sister's face. She struggles to speak. 'When we read Dad's letter, I didn't think things could get any worse. That there would be anything more awful we'd have to learn. But now there is.'

I nod my head and bite my lower lip.

'You're wrong, Dom,' Flint says, somehow calm. 'You've never been more wrong. Gil is not Kingfisher.' He pauses, his face still, his expression hard. 'But…there are twenty of them in this house. They're armed, and I haven't figured us a way out of here yet. I will, but I can't see it yet.'

Charley swallows. 'You really think we can get away?'

'Yeah,' he says. 'But until then…Dom's right. We have to join the Disciples. We have to…play their game a while until we can escape.'

I'd like to believe Flint can find an escape, that we have more than one option. I nod in agreement. 'We have to play their game for a while.'

'What? We've got to act some horrible, vicious part.' Charley looks away, her lower lip trembling.

'Yes, but that's all it is,' Flint says. 'An act. It's not who we are. We'll never really become Disciples, not inside.'

My sister turns to him, her eyes wide. 'No,' she says. 'We won't. That's *our* truth.' Her gaze meets mine.

'No, of course we won't,' I agree.

We stand there for several long minutes, silent, taking in our new reality. Then Flint checks his watch. 'We'd better go back down.' He leaves the loft first. My sister lingers; I sense there's something she wants to say.

'*Gil's a very dangerous man.*' I hear her in my head.

I don't answer, I know.

'*He threatens us all, but you most, Dom. Remember my dream. He wants you.*'

I stand very still. I want to remind her a dream is just a dream, but that probably doesn't matter.

'I'll be careful,' I say aloud. I don't accept I'm in any more jeopardy than her or Flint.

CHAPTER 15

Two months earlier

Charley's dream disturbed her. It was part of everything that happened in Scotland. A place I never really believed we were safe in. As we sat on the train going north, I was flooded with fear, convinced someone would recognise us; our pictures had been in the papers just two days before. Each station we stopped at, I expected the police to be waiting for us. But that didn't happen. Instead, we got to the Highlands safely. Charley and Flint settled in quickly, but I never felt at home.

'It's beautiful here,' Charley said. She looked out at the sun setting on the loch. 'I can't think of anywhere else I'd rather be.'

It was late, almost ten thirty, but being so far north the sun was only now setting.

'Yeah.' Flint sighed, satisfied. He stood near her; both their faces were serene.

'When you two stand together like that,' I said, 'with the hills in the distance, you'd make a great shot for a tourist brochure.' They looked like a couple, and that didn't make me feel good. 'We should get back, before it gets too dark.'

We were staying in a campsite we'd picked for its privacy rather than its facilities. There was no street lighting – there weren't even streets. You had to get back before dark or face stumbling and losing your way with a torch. We'd bought a tent, the cheapest we could find that took the three of us. When we lay down it was a squeeze; whenever you turned someone was breathing in your face. We'd been there two weeks.

Although our English accents were noticeable, we successfully stuck to set responses when people asked about us. There were a few times I almost slipped up, mentioning our real names or referring to Charley as my sister, but most of the time I managed to be Luke. More tourists were arriving each day, and Flint said that was a good thing. Yet I was worried we'd stay too long and somebody would catch on.

'I'm finding it hard to relax,' I confessed, when we were back in our tent. I lay in my sleeping bag next to Charley. Flint lay on her other side; she didn't mind being in the middle. 'You look at that loch,' I continued, 'and you feel safe, but I don't.'

'Oh, Dom,' Charley said, as though she wished I could be different.

'We're in the most beautiful place,' Flint said gently, 'far away from everything. There's nothing to worry about. Really, we're safe. Chill.'

'Flint, you're always so sure of yourself, like nothing could go wrong.'

''Cause right now, it can't.'

'Dom, what's going on?' Charley asked. She knew me better than Flint. I wasn't happy. I paused before continuing.

'I miss Dad,' I said bluntly. There was a long moment's silence.

'That's okay.' She stretched out her hand to touch my face. 'I miss Dad too.'

Flint was quiet.

'I miss him telling me off,' I continued. 'I miss small, stupid things about him like the way he'd store beer tops for God knows what. I miss his cooking. I miss our home. I miss the way things felt okay when he was around.' I was breathing hard. Where had all this come from? I had no idea I felt half of it. Flint and Charley were still as I stewed in my misery.

'Let's get out of here,' Flint eventually said. 'Just you and me. Let's go for a walk.'

'It's pitch black out there.' The idea was not appealing.

'We've got a torch.' I heard him unzip his sleeping bag and start to get up. 'Come on.' He tapped my shoulder.

I felt belligerent, but I wasn't going to sleep anyway. I joined him outside. We started to retrace the route back to the loch. I remembered the last time we went off together, the night we got drunk; it couldn't be more different now.

We sat by the dark, glistening lake. I was aware of all the sounds nature made around us: buzzing, a rippling of water, the soft breath of the breeze blowing through the grass. Flint rolled himself a cigarette. He offered me one, but I turned it down. I watched the tip of his burn, a glow of orange light.

'Now,' he said, looking up, 'I think that's a new moon.'

I glanced at the sky. 'I don't know, but it looks a pretty thin moon to me.'

'Yeah, that's why it's so dark out here.'

We were quiet for a while. 'Funny,' Flint continued, 'I thought it'd be you, not Charley, who'd find it easier to settle in here.'

I remembered back to when we were first on the run. Charley was always crying. 'Yeah, you'd think so, but Charley seems okay with things.'

I could feel him watching me through the dark. He was giving me the opportunity to say whatever it was I needed to say.

'We don't really talk about emotions, do we, Flint?'

'There's nobody said we can't.'

I realised I was afraid of saying what I wanted to out loud. Still, he was listening. 'I miss Dad, Flint,' I said again. 'I didn't know it could hurt this much. Every day it grinds away in me, and I can't let go of…' I stopped. He wouldn't want to hear this.

'Can't let go of what?' he asked softly.

I took a deep breath before continuing. 'I can't let go of wanting things to be different. I can't let go of…Kingfisher. Of Gil Zimmerman. It occupies my mind.'

Flint took his time responding. 'If it matters that much, Dom, then you should try and find him.'

I was still. I wasn't expecting that response.

'Will you help me?' I asked.

'No.' He shook his head. 'You know my feelings about it, but…I can respect you've gotta do what you've gotta do.'

I was very still. My brain ached. Flint was letting me know it wasn't him who was stopping me. I was struggling. I had permission to do something…I didn't have the guts to do.

'Shit.' I let out a miserable sigh. 'I'm…I'm not brave enough.'

'Or stupid enough,' he added for consolation. We were quiet.

'You know what you need, don't you?' he said, his voice brighter.

'What?'

'To get laid.'

I shook my head. 'Flint, not everything comes down to sex.'

'Sometimes it does,' he said. 'All that pent-up energy in you sure is looking for release. I swear, one girl and a few good shags, and you'll feel a whole lot better.'

I laughed. I couldn't help it; it was impossible to be angry with Flint for long.

'All we've gotta do, Dom, is find you a girl.' He chuckled.

'We're in the middle of nowhere.' I wasn't holding out much hope.

'Yeah, but sometimes when you least expect it is when you find it,' he promised.

We stood up to go. The tension in my body had lessened. Flint was right. It felt a long time since I'd had normal, regular concerns, thinking about things like sex. I made the decision to put Kingfisher to the back of my mind. I almost let it go.

Chapter 16

It started to rain and didn't stop. Charley began to crack. She couldn't bear the tent anymore. The ground turned to mud and almost everything we had was dirty with it.

'We can't go on like this,' she moaned. 'Flint, you've got to do something.'

'I can't stop the rain,' he said plainly.

'I like my creature comforts,' she wailed. 'I need to be dry. I want to be clean. We've got to find somewhere to stay that's made of brick.' She started to cry, which in turn prompted Flint to come up with a solution. I didn't have such power over Flint.

'Okay, this is what I suggest,' he said. I listened, wondering how he was going to satisfy Charley. 'Remember that walk we took, the really long one up those hills, there was a cottage there I'm sure was for rent. Dom and I'll go back and check it out. It looked basic so it should be cheap. You stay in the pub today and keep dry.'

My sister stopped crying as quickly as she'd started. 'I like that idea. Would you do that?' She turned to me.

'I'll go with Flint.' I was happy to get out of the tent too.

It took us two hours to trek to the cottage and back. We got the contact number. Not only did the cottage look cheap, but it was isolated. It would give us the privacy we needed. We called the owner. He ran the grocery store in the village and we went over to introduce ourselves. He was a middle-aged, stocky man. His face was round, his cheeks slightly red.

'It's not easy to get to,' he said gruffly, 'if you don't have a car.' We'd told him we didn't.

'That's okay,' Flint said. 'We like walking.'

'It needs some attention,' he continued. 'You'll have seen better.'

The bloke seemed strangely belligerent, like he didn't actually want to rent it. Or maybe he was suspicious of us. I suddenly sensed we needed to back off.

'Jake,' I said, turning to Flint, 'we should go.' Not all the Scots liked the English, and Flint was black, but I was more concerned he'd recognised our faces, that he remembered them from the papers.

A young woman came over; she'd been working in the shop. She stood by the owner and looked at us. In particular, she looked at me. Her brown eyes glistened. Now I was feeling really nervous.

'What do you think?' The man turned to her. He exaggerated the movement of his lips when speaking. 'They want to move into the cottage.'

There was a brief pause. 'Probably okay.' She had an unusual-sounding voice. Then he moved his hands in what I recognised as sign language. She was deaf. Now I was intrigued. I didn't know much about sign language except that it looked like a secret code. She signed back and he let out a long sigh.

'Alright,' he said, 'you can have it. You've got my daughter to thank.'

She was looking at me again. Her eyes seemed to smile. We were probably a similar age. She wasn't particularly pretty but then she wasn't ugly either, with her shoulder-length dark hair and slim body. I felt myself blush.

'We'd like to move in straight away,' my sister chirped in.

Gregory, as he invited us to call him, took us to the cottage in his pickup truck. He was right about the place needing attention.

It hadn't been inhabited properly for years. There was hot water and a working oven, but no heating. The whole place needed to be done up; floorboards looked about to give way and the once white walls were differing shades of grey. He wanted two weeks' rent in advance. I was shocked at how much he was charging; it wasn't worth it, but Charley's expression insisted it was. We paid him.

'I'll get Mary to pop round with a few things,' he said, making his way out the door. 'She'll bring you a box of fruit and veg, some provisions from the shop. Consider that included in the rent.' It was a last-minute concession. He got into his truck and drove off. We all stood in what would just pass as a kitchen.

'I'm not sure about any of this.' I was finding it hard to be positive.

'Look, we're dry and I want to sleep in a bed tonight.' Charley's mind was made up. 'This is a palace compared to a rained-on tent full of mud.' She went quickly up the rickety stairs to claim one of the two bedrooms.

Flint and I stood still, listening to her move above us.

'Good job Mary fancied you,' Flint said. 'It got us the cottage.'

'Nobody fancies me.'

He smiled. 'That's not what it looked like to me. I reckon you'll get shagged after all.'

I shook my head, no. We went upstairs and agreed to share a bedroom. There wasn't really much choice; my sister had commandeered the other one. It seemed a lot was going her way these days, whereas I felt listless and bad tempered most of the time.

'Of course,' I said to Flint as we unpacked. Everything was damp and smelly. 'We can't hang out here for long. That guy's charging us a fortune…it'll eat up too much money.'

'Yeah,' he agreed. 'We're going to have to do something. Our best bet will be to find some casual work round here, like with a farmer, offering to help out and at least get paid in kind.'

I looked round the room, clocking up everything that was wrong with it. 'So, you mean, we could ask Gregory if he'll let us stay here while we fix it up?'

'Something like that. Yeah. That's a good place to start.' He nodded at me; I'd got something right.

We could hear my sister humming in the other room. Some old pop song she liked.

'Maybe we need to go back to London,' I said, surprising myself. 'I think we're going to stay here too long. The longer we stay, the less safe it is.'

Flint looked at me. 'It won't be any easier in London. It could be worse. And…I'm not sure your sister feels the same way.'

'And of course, you always take Charley's side, don't you?'

'I'm not taking sides, Dom. I just want us to make the right decisions.'

'But whatever she wants, she happens to get,' I said, feeling increasingly argumentative.

'What she wants makes sense,' he replied pointedly.

'At least to the two of you.' Some part of me really wanted a fight.

Flint shook his head then turned away from me. He continued unpacking. 'You sure are hard work these days,' he said under his breath.

'Is that what you think?' I demanded.

'Your sister thinks it too,' he said very quietly, still not looking at me.

'Fuck you,' I replied, my lower lip trembling. I didn't know what to do, there wasn't anywhere else to go, and I could hear it starting to rain again.

I closed my eyes and flopped back on my bed. I could feel the springs in the mattress, but there was no point saying it. I realised how tired I was. Fed up and tired. If I couldn't stop feeling the way I did, at least sleep was an escape. Flint continued to move quietly round the room. I listened to the rain battering the cottage until everything went quiet.

I woke later. My body felt cold and stiff. The light outside was even greyer; I must have slept for hours. I went downstairs. Flint and Charley were sitting quietly in the kitchen playing cards.

'You okay?' Charley asked softly.

I shrugged. 'Still tired.'

'Well, you were out cold,' she said with a smile.

Then I spoke directly into her head. *Flint said you find me hard work.*

'Dom.' She sighed. *'Don't be stupid. We always love each other.'*

It struck me that didn't answer the question. I hated the idea her feelings were more in tune with Flint than with me.

'What you playing?' I asked aloud.

'Well,' she said, 'we found some games. There's a chess board with all the pieces, and draughts, only some of them are missing. And then these cards…'

'Black Jack,' Flint said, getting to the point. 'We're gambling with carrots.' He indicated a box near the door I hadn't noticed. 'Mary popped by.'

'Really?' I hadn't heard a thing.

'She kind of surprised us,' Charley admitted.

I walked over to the box; there was a generous amount of food in it.

'Hey,' I said, 'some of this stuff needs to go in the fridge.' How did they miss that? I started to unpack the necessary items, milk, ham and cheese, and put them in the fridge.

'She asked where "the other one" was.' Flint turned to me and winked. 'You'll need to be around next time she comes by. Give her some time, it could help us.'

'If I choose to make friends with someone it has to be genuine,' I told him.

'Then make it genuine.'

I changed the subject. 'I'm going to make some dinner.' I bent down to look in the box again. It was only then I realised my hands were shaking. I had no idea why, except I suddenly sensed something had changed. That afternoon, for Charley and Flint, something had changed.

CHAPTER 17

Two days later, Mary turned up with another delivery. She drove her father's pickup truck; it screeched to a halt and I opened the door. She smiled, holding out a small bag of fruit and veg.

'Thanks,' I said, taking it and glancing inside.

We stood a while on the doorstep. She kept staring at me; it felt unnerving. I wondered if she had something a bit missing, because I didn't think it was normal to keep staring at someone like that. I started to close the door.

'You're called Luke, aren't you?' she asked. Her voice was distinctive; it had an unusual inflection.

I nodded. 'Yeah.'

'I like that name,' she said. 'It's a good name. Do you want to come and see the otters?'

'The what?' I looked down.

'You need to speak clearly and face me when you talk,' she instructed. 'Otherwise I can't read your lips.'

'I'm…sorry,' I said, raising my eyes.

'Do you want to come and see the otters? They're not easy to find, but I know where they are. There's a mother and two cubs.'

I hesitated. Did I want to go with Mary? Not really, but then, an evening with Charley and Flint was predictable. I'd spent every one with them for weeks.

'Okay,' I replied slowly. I'd try something different.

Her face opened in a bright smile. She didn't make any effort to hide the fact she liked me. I went and got my jacket, mentioning briefly to Charley I was off out with Mary.

She drove her father's truck fast, taking the corners with a wide sweep. I tried not to think about oncoming cars. We arrived in an area I didn't know. If I'd thought the loch we had previously been at was secluded, it was nothing compared to this. We stood before the lake. There wasn't another car or person to be seen.

'This way.' She pointed. She took a rug and binoculars out of the back of the truck. A hundred metres from the water's edge, she spread out the rug and sat on it. I moved to sit beside her. It had been a long time since I'd been alone with a girl.

'You need to stay quiet and still,' she instructed.

I watched her face as she scanned the area with her binoculars. It didn't look like she could see them. We stayed sitting there. We didn't talk and barely moved. Time slowed. I had an increasing desire to fidget. How long were we going to be there? There was no way I could make my own way back. I felt uncomfortable.

Suddenly, she held the binoculars very close to her face. She'd spotted something. She moved them to my eyes and pointed to where I should look. I could see the water's edge: grass, mud and stone. Then there was a slither of movement. The mother otter was in the loch. Two cubs' heads rippled through the water behind her. Something quickened inside me. I followed their movement. They clambered out onto the bank. Mary nudged my arm, she wanted another look. She took the binoculars again, traced the otters' movements, then handed them back to me. This time the two cubs were playing, tugging on each other's fur, friendly fighting. They made me chuckle and she giggled at my response.

'Good?' she said, smiling at me.

I looked again but they had gone. 'That was good,' I told her. Something about the otters had made me happy. They were playful. 'Thanks.' I was genuinely glad she'd brought me.

'I love this place,' she said. 'When I was wee my dad used to bring me here a lot. We'd sit for hours just watching.'

A thought crossed my mind. 'Have you ever seen a kingfisher?' I let the question drop with ease.

'No.' She shook her head. 'It's too cold up here for kingfishers.'

'Okay.'

'The weather in winter's tough. They're amazing birds but they're not round here.'

She knew more about the natural world than I was ever likely to. 'Have you always lived here?'

'Uh-huh.' She nodded.

'Do you like it?' I asked, then realised it was a pretty stupid question.

'I don't know any different.' She shrugged. Of course not.

We got up and started to walk back to the truck. This time, I carried the rug for her. We got inside and I shivered. I hadn't realised how cold I was getting, watching the otters. I waited for her to start the engine, but instead she just sat back in the driver's seat.

'Can I ask you something?' she said. 'Do you have a girlfriend?'

I considered telling her yes, then decided I was fed up with lying. 'No.'

'Me neither,' she said. 'I don't have a boyfriend. I grew up with all the boys round here. I know them too well.'

She was honest, that was clear. I couldn't decide if I found her embarrassing or just very real. And her eyes – she looked at me with such intensity.

'And…have you ever had sex?' she asked bluntly.

I paused a long moment. I wasn't in a hurry to answer that.

'I've not,' she continued, 'but I'd like to.' She turned to look out the window. 'Some day,' she added. I could only feel relief she'd stopped looking at me. I didn't respond. I couldn't.

We sat there a few long minutes until she turned the key in the engine and drove us back to the cottage.

'Would you like to see the otters again?' she asked as I stepped down from the truck. Her face was open, her eyes bright.

'Maybe.' I shrugged indifferently.

'Good.' She smiled.

I watched her drive away. I closed the front door behind me, letting out a long sigh. I had never met someone so socially awkward; there were things you just didn't say. I wouldn't be seeing her again.

There was no delivery for the next three days. Our stocks ran low and we realised how useful they'd been; it made the rent more reasonable. The prospect of striking a deal with Gregory became increasingly attractive. We needed to consider when to speak to him, but I was aware of something else. Each night around six o'clock, I was listening out for that pickup truck. I didn't want to admit it, but I was thinking of Mary.

She kept coming into my thoughts. I wasn't sure why. She was blunt and honest, almost embarrassing, and I'd wondered if she wasn't quite all there, but that wasn't true. She'd just grown up in a small, sheltered world, which might make anyone naïve and out of touch, but she could sign and lip-read; she understood enough. Did she go to a local school or one catering for deaf children? I thought about that, and imagined what would have happened if she'd come to my school in London. I would probably have viewed her quite cruelly. She would quickly have been dubbed an outsider and found herself being bullied. She would be easy to pick on. That made me uncomfortable, knowing I wouldn't have been kind. I was always concerned about looking good, hanging out with the right people, never being associated with those who were looked down upon. For the first time, I almost felt relief I wasn't in London. I could be somebody else now.

On the fourth evening, the pickup truck arrived. I was playing solitaire at the kitchen table and acted like I'd not heard it. There was a knock at the door.

'You get it,' I said to Flint as casually as I could.

He opened the door and I heard Mary hand over the box. Flint moved to put its contents in the fridge. I sensed Mary standing there.

'Luke,' she called out. 'Are you going to come and see the otters again?'

Flint, whose back was turned to her, chuckled at me. 'Oh, Luke,' he teased, 'I don't want you going out with no woman when you got to stay in and make us our dinner.'

Suddenly, he was intensely annoying. I couldn't be around him.

'Okay,' I said, getting up. I walked out of the cottage and got into the pickup truck. I was thinking less about Mary and more about getting away from Flint.

We drove out to the loch again. It was still deserted. I reckoned it was too far beyond the regular tourist routes. We got down from the truck and sat near the water. This time, though, the otters must have been elsewhere. I let out a long sigh. I was disappointed, but I also felt an idiot. What was I doing there?

'Look.' She pointed up, excited. The binoculars were tight against her face. 'Osprey.'

In the distance, I saw a large bird emerging out of the dull sky. She passed the binoculars to me. I focused on the powerful brown and white bird.

'Amazing,' Mary said as it flew closer. Its wingspan was enormous and its attention fixed on the lake. I passed the binoculars back to Mary. The osprey suddenly dived down, hit the water's surface and flew up again with a fish in its claws. It was over in seconds, but something about the bird's obvious strength, agility, and sheer killer instinct grabbed me.

'Wow! That's impressive.' I'd never seen a bird of prey in action before.

'You don't get to see them often.' Mary shook her head. 'I've never seen one at this loch…I reckon you bring me luck.'

I turned to her, she smiled.

'I'd do anything to have power and strength like that bird,' I said. It struck me I'd be fearless. Nothing would hold me back.

'Would you?'

'Yeah. A bird of prey like that, it knows what it wants, and it gets it. That was like watching a missile come out of the sky.'

'You could ask it to give you some of its strength,' she said matter-of-factly. 'If it's feeling generous, it might lend you some.'

I looked at her a long moment. 'Mary, that's the craziest thing anyone's ever said to me.'

'Is it? I don't think it's crazy. It's common sense.'

'How can a bird give you its strength?' I asked, sceptical.

'Ask it, and you'll find out,' she said sincerely. 'It's got a dynamic energy – focus on that. We've all got spirit, and sometimes we share it.'

I paused. That osprey had been awesome, and for a moment I considered doing what she suggested. We were in the middle of nowhere; it wasn't like anyone was watching. I stood up slowly and opened my arms wide.

'Oh, osprey,' I called out loudly. 'Please will you give me some of your strength…your bird of prey power and majesty.' But then I started laughing. I couldn't take it seriously.

'You don't ask like that,' Mary scolded. 'There's no point if you don't ask with heart and true intention.' She wasn't impressed.

'I'm sorry.'

'Well,' she said disparagingly, 'you've blown it with the osprey now.'

'Probably,' I agreed.

We were quiet. She looked away, and I feared I'd upset her. I didn't mean to do that. I sat down beside her again.

She eventually broke the silence. 'Sometimes I ask the eagle for strength, for some of its spirit. To help me through things like when my mum died.' She turned to me, her face pensive. There was nothing to tease now.

'When did your mum die?' I asked softly.

'A few years ago. Cancer. I miss her every day.'

'I'm sorry,' I said, sensing her sadness.

'She's the one who taught me how to lip-read and sign.' Mary was upset talking about it. 'She was very special, my mum, she never let you feel bad.' Her eyes clouded with tears.

'You must really miss her.' I thought of Dad. He was special too.

'Aye, I do.' She paused. 'Sometimes, I feel very lonely.'

I nodded.

'Do you ever feel lonely?' she asked, her eyes searching mine.

'Yeah,' I admitted, 'sometimes I feel lonely.' I thought of Charley and Flint, and all we'd gone through and how hard it was. 'Sometimes I feel very alone.'

We were both quiet. Her eyes were bright. 'I hate feeling lonely,' she said with anger. Her gaze didn't move from mine.

'Yes,' I agreed.

She turned away. I sensed she hadn't finished – there was more she wanted to say.

'Would you like to kiss?' she asked plainly, turning to me again.

'Kiss?'

'Yes…but…maybe you don't find me attractive?'

'No,' I eventually answered. 'I wouldn't say that.' I paused. 'I…I think you're pretty.'

I realised it was the start of something else between us.

CHAPTER 18

Mary and I walked back to the pickup truck. We got inside and sat there for a while, silent. The sun set.

'I've never kissed anyone before,' she said.

'That's okay.' Then before we could think about it anymore, I moved quickly to place my lips on hers. I wasn't that experienced, but I knew doing it was more important than talking about it. It felt awkward at first – I almost stopped – but then we got the hang of it. We moved slowly to kissing with tongues; that turned me on. Finally, we stopped.

'We're not going any further, are we?' she said, her breathing quick.

'No.' My heart was pounding in my chest. I couldn't believe how good kissing Mary made me feel. She was soft and sweet, and I knew if I wanted I could push her further, but I wasn't going to behave like that.

We drove back without talking. I looked across at her face. Her eyes were focused on the road. Her skin was pale and smooth, her dark hair fell in soft waves to her shoulders. I hadn't thought Mary attractive before, but I did now. When we reached the cottage she switched off the engine. It was dark outside, and she put on the truck's interior light. She turned to me.

'Where *do* you come from, Luke?' she asked.

'London,' I replied truthfully.

'Will you…will you be going back to London soon?'

I couldn't answer. I had no idea where we'd go in the future.

'Because…I hope you don't go back to London soon.'

'No,' I said softly.

Her face looked sad and beautiful. I traced her left cheek with my finger. I almost kissed her again. Instead, I started to get down from the truck. She signed something.

I shook my head. 'I don't understand sign language.'

'I was saying,' she told me, 'spelling…' She smiled. 'I'm happy.'

I smiled back. 'I'm happy too.' She grinned.

I watched her drive off then went inside. The cottage was silent. Flint and Charley must have gone to bed. I took the stairs two at a time and turned the door handle carefully. I didn't want to wake Flint, not for him to tease me or ask questions. I knew something had changed tonight, something good had happened, and I wanted to keep it to myself. I gazed through the fuzz of darkness, but Flint's bed was empty.

'Flint?' I whispered.

There was no reply. I didn't understand; it was pitch black outside and there was nowhere for him to go. Had something happened? I moved down the corridor to my sister's room, suddenly anxious they'd both gone. I eased her door open. I saw her sleeping peacefully, which was a relief. But then I noticed Flint beside her. It took a few long moments for me to register what that meant. My sister and cousin were in the same bed.

The blood began to drain from my limbs. I rushed to the bathroom and vomited down the toilet. This couldn't be happening. No. Never. Not between Charley and Flint. They were cousins. They couldn't have sex; it broke all the rules. It split our world in two. It meant they were together and I was on the outside.

I couldn't breathe, I needed air. I had to get out of there. I clattered down the stairs and slammed the front door loudly behind me. Now I understood why Flint always took Charley's side. No wonder they were both happy and agreed on all the decisions made. I was alone, the only one trying to make sense of my father's wishes, trying to pursue Kingfisher.

The air outside was freezing. It felt much colder than when I'd been with Mary. And I couldn't see a thing, I'd left without a torch but I wasn't going back. I knew enough to retrace the road we'd just driven down; it meant walking into wilderness, but I didn't care. The landscape mirrored my feelings: savage, dark and empty. I was walking through darkness because it was what I'd been doing anyway. It was where Flint and Charley had been pushing me. I hoped they'd wake up and feel sick with what they'd done, because I didn't care if I never saw them again.

A burst of sound. Gunshot. For a few seconds I couldn't move, then I threw myself on the ground. My mind cleared, alert to danger. I lay motionless, silent, listening. There were more shots. They weren't as close as I'd first thought, but it was unmistakably gunshot. I dared to raise my head a fraction. I was in a ditch at the side of the road, fields on either side. I knew people shot deer and grouse, but this couldn't be hunting, not at night in the dark.

My ears slowly adjusted. The shooting came closer. I froze, my breath caught in my throat. There were muffled voices and thuds on the ground. Somebody was shouting, the tone of their voice commanding. Had I walked into some kind of military exercise? The army might do this kind of thing at night. It was a remote area and they wouldn't be disturbing anyone. I tuned into the thump of running feet, more shouts, orders. I was right. What kind of danger did that mean we were in? The army was here. They would have seen our pictures. Perhaps they were even looking for us? I could barely control my panic. If they found me in that ditch…

Car lights shone dimly through the darkness. At first they were in the distance, but then they drew nearer. In a few moments, whatever the vehicle was would pass me lying at the side of the road. Things were going from bad to worse. I had to get away but if I stood and ran, I'd be seen. My only option was to squeeze as tightly as I could into the ditch. If I was absolutely still, it was possible nobody would notice me. The headlights grew larger, coming closer; they didn't belong to a car but a truck. It looked like a military vehicle. I held my breath as it passed, afraid my heartbeat was audible. I waited, expecting the truck to stop and for someone to come back and get me. That didn't happen. Instead, it continued ahead and stopped further along the road. A door opened and someone got down.

'Hey.' It was a woman's voice. There was the sound of running. 'How did it go?'

'We need to be fitter,' a man replied.

I was confused. It didn't sound right. I thought the army was all 'yes, sir,' 'no, sergeant,' and screaming at soldiers by their surnames.

'We really need to be fitter,' the man repeated. 'We've got to increase our training if we're going to succeed.' There was a pause.

'Yeah.' Another man's voice came in. 'We've got to get out more. Gil's going to have to decide what the greater risk is: being caught out training or screwing up an operation because we're not strong enough.'

'I'll report back,' the first man said firmly, asserting his authority. 'Then Gil and I will make the right decision.'

'We'd better go.' It was the woman again. 'It'll be light soon.'

I heard what sounded like people clambering into the truck. The engine started, the wheels moved; it was doing a three-point turn. That meant it was going to be driving back my way. I shrank as far as I could into the corner of the road. The lights came towards me. I felt them bright on my body, but the truck continued moving on. I only dared raise my head once it had gone. There was a tingling sensation in my hands and feet. I'd heard his name. He was here. Gil. This wasn't the army. Quite without intention, I'd discovered the Disciples.

CHAPTER 19

Charley looked tired and anxious. She interrogated me. 'Where have you been?'

I'd made it back. They were both waiting in the kitchen.

'We need to talk.' I shivered. I was freezing, but too pumped up with adrenalin to care. Outside, the sun was beginning to rise. 'I know what you and Flint are up to, and I've something important to say.'

There was a pause; you could cut the tension in the room with a knife.

'It's not what you think,' Flint said carefully.

'What?' I snapped. 'You're sleeping with my sister. You've wanted to shag her from the moment you saw her, and now you've got your way.'

'I love Charley,' Flint said, 'so don't talk like that.'

I swallowed and shook my head. 'Flint, you don't know what love is.'

His expression hardened. I was pushing him, but he'd come between my sister and me. Now things were too important.

'It's sick, what you're doing together. You're cousins. It's incest!' I slammed my point home.

'Stop it, Dom,' Charley interjected.

'It's not incest.' Flint spat the word out. 'We're cousins through love, not blood. We're not *brother* and sister.' What was he trying to imply?

There was a dangerous energy between us. We were going to fight.

'Shut up!' Charley shouted. 'Both of you, stop it!' She stood between Flint and me. She knew we were about to hit each other. Her eyes glared at me.

I spoke into her thoughts. '*You betrayed me.*'

'Dominic,' she replied aloud, 'you're my brother, I love you. We need to talk.' Somehow, she kept calm. She turned to Flint. 'Can you leave us alone a while?'

Flint looked back at me. He wasn't happy to go.

'I need to speak to Dom on my own,' Charley continued, placating him. 'Please.'

After a few moments, he left the room. Charley and I were alone. She pulled out a chair and sat down at the table. She indicated I join her.

'Will you listen to me, Dom?' she asked, her eyes begging me to understand.

'You betrayed me, Charley.' It was all I could say.

She shook her head, no. She looked close to tears.

'You did,' I said, but I was finding it hard to be angry with her. I just felt upset. 'You went with Flint and pushed me out. Everything's gone your way. You've no idea how that's made me feel. We were meant to stick together. How could you have slept with him, your own cousin?'

'Dominic, you think things are simple but they're not. Would you just listen to me?'

I sat down opposite her.

'When we were at school,' she said softly, 'I was never really attractive. I always knew nothing would happen there, not in terms of boyfriends or sex or anything like that. I used to think maybe, if I'm lucky, it will happen at university, that's what

I hoped for. And I always expected you to come home one night, after a party, and you'd tell me how you got off with some girl, and one thing led to another, and you'd had sex. That's how I thought it would happen – you'd have sex first. Then everything fell apart. No school. No university. No future as we'd hoped for.' She stopped, her eyes sad.

'He's still your first cousin, Charley,' I said, although I felt the hurt she was expressing.

'Flint's not what you think, and he loves you, Dom.'

I shook my head. 'He's slept with lots of girls. You said it yourself once – "Don't think I don't know what he's about." But you just went ahead and gave him what he wanted.'

'I went to him, Dom,' she said slowly. 'He was worried about *you*, and your response, but I went to him.'

I couldn't reply; everything felt mixed up in my head. She could see I was upset.

'That first day when we came here, and you were arguing with everyone and then went to bed…that's the day it started. I suddenly realised I had no sense of the future. We could be picked up tomorrow and tortured, and I realised more than anything I wanted to know something about sex, and something about love, and I was crying. Flint tried to comfort me and then I let it happen. I made it clear what I wanted.'

I closed my eyes. 'Stop.' I was feeling sick again.

'Don't be angry, Dom,' she said gently. 'Can't you see? *We* love you. That hasn't changed. Just because we're sleeping together doesn't mean we don't both love you.'

'Except you've pushed me out.' I opened my eyes and looked her straight in the face. 'That doesn't feel like love.'

'How?' She genuinely didn't understand.

'Can't *you* see, Charley? You and Flint agree on everything. All the decisions go your way. I'm just this person you have to put up with. I don't get a say.'

'What is you want, Dom? What is it you want us to do that we're not already doing?'

She really didn't get it, but I felt how much she wanted to be my sister, a good sister to me.

'Kingfisher,' I whispered.

Charley grew very still. 'Dom, I thought you'd given that up.'

'Listen to me,' I said, 'very carefully. I discovered something last night. The Disciples are here.' The words had been spoken. Both of us were silent. Then I told her what had happened. 'We came here,' I said, 'because we thought it would be isolated, with independent-thinking people minding their own business. Well, that's why they're here too.' I waited while she took it all in.

'We need to talk about this,' she said. 'All of us. Together. And what it means.'

'No. We're our father's children. First, you and I talk about it. Nobody else.'

Her breath quickened. I was challenging her. I was asking her to leave Flint out.

'I'm scared,' she said. 'It's terrifying, if what you've said is true.' Then, although she didn't say it aloud, I heard her thoughts. *If Gil Zimmerman is Kingfisher, what might happen if we make contact with him?*

'I'm scared too.' I spoke directly into her mind. *'But I don't think we should let that stop us.'*

'They're terrorists, Dom. They're dangerous people.' We were talking now only through our thoughts. *'I was beginning to feel safe. I don't want to get involved with them.'*

'Charley, think, perhaps this is our fate? Dad left us that message for a reason. He wanted us to seek them out and now they're here.

We thought we could avoid them, but they're here. Don't you see?' I stressed. *'We could be very close to a truth we might otherwise never know.'*

'If we make contact with the Disciples, nothing will ever be the same again.' She stopped, anxious. I waited. *'I need time to think about it.'*

Finally, it was a move in my direction. *'Okay,'* I said gently. *'Think about it, but not for long. And while you do, we keep this to ourselves.'*

'I don't like not telling Flint.'

'We're not going to not tell him, we're just not telling him until we've thought this through ourselves.' I hoped I sounded reasonable. *'We need to know what we want first. It's delaying a discussion, that's all.'*

She was quiet a long moment. *'Okay.'*

I nodded and breathed out slowly, satisfied.

'Now go and make up with Flint,' she said aloud, her voice firm.

I was closer to what I wanted.

Chapter 20

Flint and I had a chat about his relationship with my sister. I told him, honestly, I wasn't happy about it. He said, honestly, he'd feel the same way if he were me. Still, he was glad it was in the open now.

'I'd like to think you can live with it, Dom, but…I get that it freaked you out.'

It's hard to argue with someone who's being so sympathetic.

'I can live with it,' I told him, because I knew I had to. We hugged and made up. It was also clear there were other important things we had to consider.

'We've been here a while,' Flint said that evening as we worked out the money we had left. 'It's going to look suspicious if we keep paying rent without working. It's not like people go on holiday forever. I reckon…we should move on now or strike a deal with Gregory.'

Charley and I exchanged glances. We had no desire to leave. I knew about the Disciples, and Charley was comfortable in the cottage. We all agreed to meet Gregory. We'd been telling lies for a long time and now we'd just tell some more.

It was Friday evening. Gregory drew up in his pickup truck and Mary was with him. I hadn't seen her since we'd kissed, and there had been no more deliveries. As soon as they walked in, I sensed Mary was tense. That should have told me something was wrong.

'You want to discuss staying on in the cottage…reaching an agreement on the rent.' Gregory got straight to the point.

'Yeah,' said Flint. We'd decided he'd do the talking. 'When you told us it needed attention, you were right. We'd like to stay a few more weeks, but instead of paying cash, we'll do up the place for you.'

Gregory listened, but his face was impassive. 'Are you good at building renovation?' Something in his voice was teasing. He didn't believe we could do it.

'We're not offering to rewire or plumb the place,' Flint continued casually, 'but we can paint the walls, deal with some of the floorboards, improve the look. Then…you could charge more.'

Gregory looked at him coolly. 'Do you think I'm stupid?' he asked.

Flint hesitated. This wasn't what we expected. 'No,' he answered politely.

'You don't think I know what's going on,' Gregory said, withdrawing a piece of paper from his jacket pocket, 'but I do.' He unfolded it, flattened it out and then turned it to us. It was a page from a newspaper, our photos clear on it. 'Remember, I sell papers. I can even read. I know exactly who you are: Dominic and Charley Minster, and you, Flint, their cousin.'

We stood there, motionless and silent. A cold dread worked its way through my body.

'I've been wondering what to do about you,' he continued. 'I don't believe everything I read – quite the opposite. I know they'll often call a good man bad.' He paused. None of us could speak. 'And you're a similar age to my Mary, so I've been giving you the benefit of the doubt. "How bad can they be?" I've asked myself.' He posed the question bluntly.

My thoughts were scrambling, panicked, trying to make sense of what was happening. I realised it was possible he hadn't told the police yet.

'We're not bad people,' I said, somehow. 'We've done no harm.'

'If that's so…then why do they keep printing this stuff?' I felt Gregory goading me.

I realised, suddenly, the lies had to end. Only the truth could save us, if that was even possible.

'The papers are lying,' I said, holding my nerve. 'My father worked for LifeStar Corporation. He was a geneticist, and he discovered something very important, something that could be important to you, me or any other human being, but it wasn't information LifeStar Corporation wanted to get out – or the government.' I paused, he had to believe me.

'Dad said MI5 would take him, and they have, and now the papers are full of this stuff, stories denouncing him, and saying they want us. But we've done nothing wrong. We're schoolkids.' I let my lower lip tremble a little for effect. 'They've made us fugitives, but we don't know why. We've done nothing wrong,' I finished, breathless.

'LifeStar Corporation?' Gregory asked slowly. 'They don't say much about that in the papers. He was involved with the Disciples, they're holding him under terrorist legislation.'

'We don't know anything about the Disciples,' I said, my eyes fixed on him. 'My father never said anything about them, ever. He only spoke about blowing the whistle on LifeStar Corporation. The first we learnt about the Disciples was when reading the papers ourselves.' I had no idea if he believed me. I felt quite sick.

'I should call the police.'

'No,' Charley said loudly. 'They'll torture us.'

The mood in the room altered. Gregory grew very still. I felt my hands and feet tingle, I swallowed hard.

'We have reason to believe they'll torture us.' My sister's voice was breathy, afraid.

I felt rising panic. She had to stop. She was saying too much. I had told him the truth, all he needed to hear; we must reveal no more than that.

'What she means,' Flint said slowly, firmly, taking over, 'is we've done no wrong. But they're behaving like we have so we don't reckon they'll treat us well. I get you're a man who knows bullshit when you hear it,' he said respectfully. 'You figured out who we are and you're right to question that. But now, we're telling the truth. It's all we've got.'

Gregory was quiet. He took his time responding. 'You're right,' he said, his manner calculating. 'I do know bullshit when I hear it. The papers are full of it…and so is LifeStar Corporation.' He paused.

What was going on? Had I just heard him right? He thought the papers and LifeStar Corporation were full of bullshit?

'But the question I'm still left with,' he continued slyly, 'is what do I do with you?'

We were silent. I realised I was barely breathing.

'The safest thing for me to do, and in particular for Mary,' his eyes narrowed on me, 'would be to hand you over to the police. Although…I don't doubt you'd suffer in their hands.' His eyes shifted to Flint. 'I could let you go on your way, but you probably won't get that far.' He paused then dropped his voice to a whisper. 'You can't have any connection with the Disciples or they'd be providing you with some kind of protection. So that means…you're in a very vulnerable position.' He stopped. I had no idea what he'd say next.

'I hate LifeStar Corporation,' he said slowly, 'and maybe… I have enough sympathy with your situation…to consider letting you stay here.'

I struggled to take in what he was saying. I'd feared he'd be the death of us, but now, was he actually proposing he'd let us hide out in his cottage?

'Staying here would be good,' Charley whispered. She was almost crying at the possibility. Gregory's face revealed nothing. I let my eyes slide across to Mary. She was staring at me.

'I'm going to let you stay here,' he said, but his demeanour wasn't generous. I feared he was up to something. 'And you, Dominic.' He turned to me. 'If you go near my daughter again, I'll kill you. Don't think I don't know what's going on there too. You're dangerous to know, and you stay away from her.'

'Okay.' I nodded. There was no choice.

'You deal with me directly, and if the police discover you, she's innocent, unaware. Understand what I'm saying? *You never knew her,*' he stressed.

'I understand.' I couldn't blame him – he wanted to protect his daughter. He turned to Mary and signed something. She looked down and away from me.

'Why do you hate LifeStar Corporation?' Flint asked carefully.

Gregory drew in a painful-sounding breath. 'They killed my wife.'

Flint nodded like he might have expected such an answer.

'Their new cancer drug – she was part of the drug trial. They sold it to us as the great new cure, but I know…*I know,*' he stressed, 'they didn't tell us the truth about its risks. When my wife signed their consent form agreeing to take that drug, she signed her own death warrant. It was full of half-truths and lies.' His voice was bitter and full of loathing.

I dared to glance at Mary. Her eyes were blazing; she was breathing fast. They blamed LifeStar Corporation for her mother's death. It was a horrible moment as I realised their tragedy had become our saving grace. Why else would Gregory spare us? He was only doing so because of his own intense hatred of LifeStar Corporation.

'How terrible,' my sister muttered.

'I won't let you stay here long,' Gregory snapped, 'and you'd better do a good job on improving this place.'

'We'll do a good job,' Flint assured him.

'I'll pop round tomorrow with some paint.'

They left; there was nothing else to say. We listened as the engine of the truck kicked into life and they drove away.

'Jesus.' Charley gulped back a single sob. 'I thought we'd had it.'

Flint moved to comfort her and I realised I was shaking. Flint and Charley embraced and I walked over to them, feeling slightly light-headed. They each extended an arm for me to join their hug. We held each other close. I closed my eyes and felt their bodies warm against mine. We only had each other and we'd no idea for how long.

Chapter 21

The next day, Gregory came back with tins of paint and a large box of food. There was enough of both to last a while. Flint and I helped him unload and then he was gone. He wouldn't be returning soon. I felt bleak. I wouldn't be seeing Mary again, and I wasn't convinced we were safe.

We went to bed early. Sleep was a relief. But, as I was drifting off, I heard the pickup truck draw up. Flint stirred in the other bed. I got up carefully and looked out the window. It was Mary. I went downstairs and opened the door gently. I didn't want to wake the others.

'Mary, what are you doing here?' My heart quickened.

She looked at me a long moment. 'You're not called Luke?' she said, upset.

'No.' I shook my head. 'I'm Dominic.'

She was hurt; I'd deceived her.

'I lied,' I said honestly, 'but now you know why.'

'Dom-in-ic.' She enunciated my name slowly. I nodded. She moved her fingers, signing. 'That's your name,' she informed me, spelling the seven letters again with her hands.

'Yes,' I replied.

'Did you lie about the other stuff?' She probably thought I had a girlfriend.

'No.' There was a pause between us.

'I'd like to see you again.'

'That's…not a good idea. Your father…he's made his position clear.'

Her eyes clouded with tears. 'But what about my position?' Because she was upset her pronunciation weakened.

'Mary,' I said, trying to hold firm, 'I'm not going to be good for you. I'm in trouble, we're fugitives. We're on the run.'

'I don't care.' A single tear worked its way down from her left eye.

I felt her vulnerability and loneliness. I wanted to hug her, but involving myself with Mary could threaten us all.

'Mary, if we get close…' I paused. 'If we see each other again… it won't end well. I'll be off soon and then what?'

She was shaking her head, trying not to cry.

'Please, Mary.' I felt quite desperate. 'Go home.'

She moved her hands to bring my face to hers. We kissed. It felt hot and intense.

'I'm happy when I'm with you,' she whispered. 'I'm going to find a way to see you.'

I closed my eyes. I couldn't look at her. I had to insist, no, but the words wouldn't come. Instead, I opened my eyes again. She was smiling.

She went back to the truck, got inside and started the engine. Even as she drove away, she didn't take her eyes off me.

'Oh, shit.' I slowly closed the door.

'Trouble?' A soft voice sounded behind me. I jumped; it was Flint. How long had he been there?

'I've no idea what I do,' I confessed, anxious now Mary had gone.

'How about enjoy yourself?' His expression was playful.

'Flint, aren't you bothered? About Gregory and what he could do to us?'

He shrugged. 'What makes you think Gregory will ever know?' He smiled. 'She likes you and you like her. He's a jealous old git. He won't know anything, she'll see to that.' He spoke with confidence, like nothing could go wrong.

In the days that followed, I couldn't get Gregory out of my mind, and not just because of Mary. We started painting our way round the cottage, but why was he *really* letting us do this? He had an agenda – just not one I could figure out. And his words ran round my thoughts: 'You can't have any connection with the Disciples or they'd be providing you with some kind of protection.'

Of course – he got it. Flint and Charley struggled with the concept, but Gregory understood something I'd not been able to articulate. The Disciples provided protection to those involved with them. It was part of the trade-off. They couldn't protect my father now, but they might protect us; that was why Dad was guiding us to them. I had to speak to Charley. We couldn't delay any longer.

The following night, I waited until I heard Flint snoring in his bed.

'Charley,' I whispered as I opened her door.

She wasn't asleep. 'I keep going over things in my head,' she said. 'I'm tired, but I can't sleep.'

'Me neither.' I edged over to her bed and got under the covers with her; the room was freezing. 'I don't think we can trust Gregory.'

'No.'

'Which means…the Disciples may be our only hope?'

'We can't contact them.' Her mind was made up, and we hadn't even discussed it.

'You've been speaking to Flint?' I tested, trying to keep my emotions in check.

'No, I've said nothing to Flint. This is about you. I had a dream…the other night…about Gil Zimmerman.'

'Yes? So?'

Her expression was troubled. 'In the dream, it wasn't good. He…he had some kind of hold over you.'

I didn't respond immediately. She was afraid, and it was affecting how she saw things. 'It was just a dream.'

'Sometimes dreams come true,' she insisted. Then I heard her thoughts. '*He wants to find us.*'

'That was in the dream too?'

'Yes,' she whispered. 'He's looking for us, Dom.'

'Isn't that good? Doesn't that show he's got something to give us? He could even protect us?'

'*He's dangerous.*' She spoke directly into my head. '*He's a danger to the three of us, but most of all to you.*'

'Why?' I said, frustrated.

'Because he wants something from you,' she continued aloud.

'What?'

She was silent.

'What?' I repeated loudly.

'*Your soul.*'

I felt winded. It was like someone had hit me in the chest. I'd never experienced such a disconcerting sensation, but, on a physical level, I knew my sister's dream was true. Neither of us spoke. Flint's words moved through my mind: 'The fishers of men's souls.' I closed my eyes, and Gil's image was behind them. I was filled again with the feeling that, somehow, I knew him.

'Do you believe me?' she asked quietly.

'Yes.' I shivered.

'We stay away from the Disciples,' she said decisively.

I couldn't respond. I felt a sudden and deep sadness. Any link to or help from my father was fading. I should move from her room back to my own, but my body was leaden.

'Can I say something else?' Charley asked carefully.

'Go on,' I said, although I didn't think I was going to like it.

'Stay away from Mary.'

'Was she in the dream too?' I checked, upset.

'No, but I know you, Dom, and I don't want you to get hurt.'

'I've got to stay away from Gil and I've got to stay away from Mary.' She wasn't being fair.

'Dom, we can't trust Gregory, so we can't trust Mary either. I want you to know love. I really want you to experience something good, but it's not her.'

I wanted to tell her Flint didn't feel the same way. Flint wanted something to happen between us. But I didn't, because Charley's concerns were closer to my own.

I got out of her bed and returned to mine. I lay still under the covers, our conversation heavy in my thoughts. I felt alone, really alone. I had no idea when that would end.

CHAPTER 22

Three nights later, we sat down to eat. It was late. We'd been painting for hours. We had a meal of soup followed by ham and cheese sandwiches. I ate absent-mindedly, unhappy. The future had diminished: there would be no help from Gil, no possibility of even trying to contact him, and I missed Mary. She wasn't like any other girl I'd met. She did crazy things like ask an eagle for its strength, but she was also real. An honest person. You couldn't be that honest and betray someone. I knew she was true. I also knew it wasn't safe to continue seeing her. I was gutted.

Halfway through eating, we heard the familiar sound of Gregory's pickup truck. It came to a halt, the door opened and someone climbed down. There were two knocks on the door. I felt my heart skip a beat but didn't look up from my meal. Charley rose to answer it.

'Can I see Dominic?' It was Mary's distinctive voice.

'I'm not sure that's a good idea,' I heard my sister answer slowly.

There was a long pause.

'Dominic,' Mary called out.

'Mary,' Charley responded quickly, 'it's best if you go home now.' She wouldn't budge from the doorway, blocking Mary's view. 'Dominic's not in.' It was a bare-faced lie, and Mary would know that.

I raised my eyes slightly and caught Flint looking at me. I could see he was surprised at Charley's response; he didn't know about our private conversation.

'Dom-in-ic!' Mary cried out, her voice distorting as she tried to shout.

Suddenly, I couldn't bear it anymore. I got up, brushed past my sister and, taking Mary's arm, walked her back towards the pickup truck. The movement was harsh.

'Mary, go home,' I instructed firmly, trying to fight my own feelings. But I had to look at her so she could read my lips and, once I did that, I was lost. Her lower lip started to tremble. I wasn't behaving well towards her.

'My dad thinks I'm at my Aunt Rosie's,' she told me. 'It took a lot to get here tonight. If he finds out I lied, he'll kill me.'

'Then you should go to your Aunt Rosie's,' I said softly.

Her eyes were wild and bright. 'Don't you want to see me?'

I gazed at her. I wished she didn't look beautiful, not tonight.

'I want to see you,' I heard myself reply. It wasn't what I should be saying. I knew where things were leading, and it couldn't end well. There was a long pause between us.

'Do you want to go to the loch?' she asked.

I nodded, yes. I couldn't speak. I followed her into the pickup truck. I didn't look back; Charley could think what she wanted. Flint would deal with her. Mary started the engine and we drove off.

The loch, when we got there, was still and glistening. We sat a while watching the sun set, a spread of orange and pink light refracting through the clouds. The sky grew darker.

'We're not going to see the otters tonight.' I exhaled.

No, we hadn't gone there to see the wildlife. I thought about what we really wanted. I turned to her, but it was too dark now inside the truck for her to lip-read. I was forced to switch on the interior light.

'You'd leave here if you could, wouldn't you?' I said, fiercely.

Her eyes brimmed with unspoken emotion. Of course she would. She wanted to get away from her father, from all that felt constrained in her life.

'I want to escape my life too,' I told her. 'I want to be free.' I pulled my top over my head. My chest was bare. It rose and fell with my quickening breath. She didn't move immediately, but then slowly raised her hand to touch me. Her fingers were cold on my skin.

'I've not done this before,' I whispered, 'but I want to do it now, with you.'

She swallowed. Her eyes didn't leave mine, but she nodded.

For a few long moments, neither of us seemed able to move. I was aware I needed to do something, to take the initiative. But then she slowly undid the zip on her jeans. She shifted awkwardly in her seat to pull them down and took her underwear with them. Her lower half was naked, her breathing growing faster. Her eyes were like those of a wild animal during a chase. I didn't want her to be afraid. I leant over and kissed her gently.

We kissed for a while, our kisses gradually growing deeper. My tongue moved in her mouth and I let my hand slip slowly between her legs. She let out a muffled noise as I touched her. What we were doing was new and intense, and I'd never felt this turned on. We moved awkwardly across the length of the truck's seat. Our breaths were quick and loud. I started to undo my belt and jeans, and together we released them over my legs. Then she wriggled below me. My heart was racing. I stretched up and switched off the light.

Afterwards, we held each other. We didn't speak, there wasn't any need to. My mind was empty of thoughts and worries. There was just Mary, the touch and feel of her warm body next to mine. I smiled and she curled up tighter into me. Eventually, she turned on the light.

'I love you,' she mouthed slowly.

'Do you?'

She moved her hands through my hair. 'Yes.' She smiled.

'You can't,' I told her softly, 'you don't really know me. You lust me, but that's something different.'

'No,' she insisted, 'and I do know you.' There was a pause between us.

'How do you know me?' I asked, and we glanced down my naked torso and giggled.

'I know the colour of your soul.'

'What?' I responded, surprised.

'The colour of your soul,' she repeated, serious.

I gazed at her beautiful face. 'You're crazy, Mary. You know that?' But I was smiling at her too.

'Don't you want to know what colour it is?'

'I guess.'

'It's blue,' she said, 'but not a dark blue, a bright one, an azure blue like…' she thought a moment '…like the blue on a kingfisher.' Her face was open, her voice bright.

I looked at her without moving or speaking. 'That's a special blue, Mary,' I eventually managed to say, 'and it's not me.' I looked away, afraid I might cry. She grew still.

'Why are you sad, Dominic?'

I couldn't begin to tell her; it would mean starting at the beginning and getting lost along the way. There was a lump at the back of my throat.

'Do you love me?' she asked, the need for reassurance in her voice.

'Yes,' I said, turning to her. 'I love you.' We smiled.

Later, we drove back to the cottage. We both knew her father would be waiting for her at home; still, she came inside a while.

Flint, thankfully, was not in the bedroom. He was with my sister, which hopefully meant he'd made her see sense. Mary and I had our privacy. We made love again. Sex was fun, a special kind of intimacy. When she left, she signed and said, 'I love you.' It was easy to sign back. We never said anything else. We didn't know when we'd meet again, so we behaved as though it was just the beginning. When I fell asleep, I was happy.

An hour later, the Disciples arrived, and everything changed forever.

CHAPTER 23

We stand before Gil. We're back in his study. He sits at the table watching us closely. Behind us, Tom hovers in the doorway, blocking it. We know, anyway; there is no escape.

'And your decision?' Gil's face is serious.

'We'll join you,' I say decisively.

'Good.' His eyes scan us. 'Good,' he repeats, and almost smiles. Tom comes into the room and stands beside him.

'Take a few days to relax and get to know us,' Gil says. 'Familiarise yourselves with the routine of the house. Then Tom will start your training regime.'

Tom nods. 'We don't generally train on this land,' he informs us. 'I'll take one or two of you out at a time for land-based exercises. Then both of you,' he says, indicating Charley and me, 'out on the sea. You can breathe underwater, but you're also going to have to swim some distance, and that requires stamina and training.'

They've known all along what they want us to do. Their manner is businesslike; there is no emotion.

'There's a gym in the basement,' Tom continues. 'I'll give each of you a programme to build up your muscle strength. It means if you're not outside, you still keep working, your training continues.'

'And although what we do is vitally important work,' Gil adds, 'we also find time to enjoy ourselves. It's how we stay sane with such an onerous task.' He pauses, summing us up. 'There's not a lot to do out here so feel free to join us in what little entertainment there is. It can get pretty intense and we let off steam when we can.' He holds me in his gaze. 'And you'll find a piano, Dominic, in the room on the far right off the corridor.'

Nothing prepared me for that. He knows I can play. What did Dad tell him?

'Thanks, but…' My voice trails off.

His eyes spark with energy. I think if he stared at paper through glass, it would ignite. Then a bell rings twice in the house.

'Lunchtime,' Tom announces, and to my relief we're dismissed.

We settle in quickly, because it ensures our survival. We play the game well. The Disciples are friendly, so much so I think they're working very hard to help us fit in. Baz spends a lot of time with Flint. He's black, in his twenties and wears his hair in short dreadlocks. They appear to get on.

'I'm not stupid,' Flint confides. 'I get what's happening. Get Baz the black guy to make friends with Flint, they'll have stuff in common, and then he'll show me how much the Disciples represent my interests.'

'Don't you think he genuinely likes you?' I ask, because it feels impossible to know.

Flint shrugs. 'Maybe…but they also want us onside.'

'Do you like him?'

Flint pauses. 'Yeah, I like him, but I shouldn't. I shouldn't trust any of them, and really, I don't.'

Charley makes friends too, or at least she creates a good impression of it. She's outgoing and sociable, which I usually am too, but here I feel withdrawn. I can't act like her or Flint. And the Disciples are physical. They high five, shake hands, wrestle and hug a lot. The guys embrace more than the girls, but I won't join them. Something in me refuses. I keep to myself.

The house's routine is well-defined and ordered. All meals are eaten communally, and the rest of the day is spent training in the gym, doing household chores or hanging around feeling bored. Nobody gets to leave the mansion except for training purposes, and that's usually when it's dark. We're on top of each other all the time, but leaving the house risks being seen, which risks the whole enterprise.

In the evening, after we've eaten, there is often some kind of lecture or discussion. Different Disciples take it in turn to lead them, focusing on a particular political issue: exploitation in the financial system; the evils of multinational companies; climate change, and the police as agents of the repressive state. The lectures always go on too long; nobody knows when to stop. I'll watch as Flint starts to nod off, yet somehow keeps his eyes open. I love him. But what I sense is important is the way these meetings reinforce the Disciples' beliefs. They always end with the same rallying call. A chorus of voices.

'We are the Disciples of Truth.'

The only one who ever holds my attention is Gil. When he speaks, I listen, engaged. Something about his energy and absolute conviction fascinates me. I can't look away. He believes in what he says – he doesn't doubt himself. He knows he's right, and if I didn't know better, I'd be convinced by him too.

Night time is the hardest. They let us sleep together in the loft, but that doesn't spare us from the interactions in the rest of the house. There are no locks on the doors, and it seems everyone has at least one or two lovers. We hear feet running between rooms. There are distant grunts and sighs, the occasional burst of laughter. People are having sex, often and noisily. I find it hard to ignore, and some of the women come on to me. I stutter, turning them down; I don't want to get close to any of them. During the day, though, there is no sign of boyfriend or girlfriend behaviour.

'We're all like brothers and sisters.' I hear their refrain. But that's not true, because brothers and sisters don't sleep with each other.

Tom starts our training. Flint throws himself into it and I follow his example. It helps deal with the boredom and anxiety I feel most of the time.

'Put it like this,' Flint says under his breath, 'I don't mind getting a great body. It'll help us get out of here.'

In training, Flint's always faster than me, and he can lift heavier weights than I can. Still, I try my best.

'I'm impressed.' Tom congratulates me after four weeks of working out. 'You're improving, and fast, but this is just the beginning.' And, of course, this has nothing to do with us, but them. They want something, and we will provide it.

'When are they taking you out on the sea?' Flint asks me later. We're alone.

'I don't know. I'm surprised they haven't already.'

He's thoughtful. 'When they do,' he says very quietly, 'it's possible you could escape. Swim off. You'll be underwater, difficult to trace.'

'I don't think it's going to happen like that,' I whisper back. This is dangerous talk.

'But if you can escape, you must,' Flint insists. 'I know Charley will say no, but you must, Dom. Both of you, if you have the chance. You have to take that opportunity.'

I shake my head slowly. 'No, Flint, it's not just Charley who feels that way.'

'I mean it,' he says, begging. 'I want you both to be safe.'

But I know even if it were possible, we would never leave him. I also realise Flint can see no way of escape. We are truly trapped.

After midnight, a week later, Tom takes Charley and me out on the sea. The wind blowing across the water is freezing, the waves choppy. We're in wetsuits, but they're a limited barrier to the cold. Baz steers the small motor boat. Tom sits beside him, armed. He doesn't take his eyes off us. They told us the gun was for our protection, but I don't think so. We stop some distance from shore. A single light illuminates the sea around us.

'In.' Tom signals for us to go overboard.

The water is like ice on our hands and faces. It almost burns, it's so cold.

'Jesus,' I gasp. Charley shivers beside me.

'This is what you've got to acclimatise to,' Tom instructs. 'Now start swimming. We'll track your movement from the boat above.'

There are fluorescent strips on our wetsuits, and electronic tags sewn into them; they have no intention of losing us. We go under the water. It is dark and murky. I strain to see Charley a few feet away. She grabs my arm, afraid of losing contact.

'*Breathe,*' I say into her mind. I know she can do it. We're the same.

Still, it is terrifying, inviting the freezing sea water into our lungs. I feel a surge of panic – I'm drowning, I can't do it. The cold water feels like a punch in my chest, but then I watch the bubbles rising out of my mouth. I'm breathing and we're underwater. Charley moves beside me, bubbles rising from her mouth. She releases her grip on my arm.

'*I'm okay,*' she says into my head.

'*Yes.*'

We swim until we can barely feel our bodies, our hands and faces numb. My limbs struggle with the cold and my own exhaustion. It takes much more effort to swim underwater than on its surface. Charley is first to go back to the boat. I watch her legs disappear as they pull her in. I follow.

'How long was that?' I ask Tom. I don't want to admit how tired I feel. My stamina's limited despite all the muscle-building exercises.

'Not long enough,' he says curtly, as the boat heads back.

I watch his face. He's not happy. We are not good enough. They want more.

Chapter 24

I can't sleep. I lie still with my eyes closed, but there is too much noise in the house, and Charley and Flint are making out. They try to be discreet, but still, I feel a loneliness I didn't know possible. My one night with Mary is like a dream now, one I can barely remember. My sister's sighs increase; I have to get out. I rise and leave the room.

I weave my way down to the kitchen. I pour out a tall glass of cold milk and take a sip. I'd drink milk at home, when I was younger; I'd drink it every day. I close my eyes and imagine I'm back in our kitchen. At this hour, my father and sister would be asleep or maybe he'd be busy in his study. Still, the noises around would be familiar and comforting.

'What you doing, Dominic?' My father might ask that. Only now it's not my father's voice. I open my eyes and turn to see Gil. Clare's by his side. He's wearing pyjama bottoms, she the top. It barely covers her private parts. I sense they've been having sex too. They seem relaxed, happy. Gil pops a few pieces of bread under the grill. Clare moves to the fridge and slices some cheese.

'Having a glass of milk,' I reply quietly.

Clare looks across at me. 'How sweet,' she says, 'like a little boy. A glass of milk.'

I feel myself blush. I don't want to be called a little boy.

Gil watches me too. 'You okay?' he asks.

I don't feel okay at all, but I can't say that. 'Charley and Flint are…' I shrug. 'You know…I thought I'd give them their privacy.' I sound reasonable.

'Ah,' Gil says with a sly smile.

I move to the couch, away from them, and sitting, rest my head back. I smell the cheese melting under the grill.

'Want some?' Clare calls over.

'No thanks,' I reply, without looking at them. I want them to go. I hear them giggle and kiss then leave. I shut my eyes. I'm so tired, I wish I could sleep and wake up in a different life.

Someone sits down beside me. I open my eyes quickly. It's Gil. He's not gone after all.

'Sometimes, I like to drink this stuff too,' he says, taking a gulp from a glass of milk.

'Okay.' I'm aware we're alone. There is nothing and no one between us; that makes me nervous. And the way he looks at me, I think he can see right through me. How does he do that?

'You know, Dominic, you don't have to be this alone.'

'What?' My breath catches.

'I mean,' he says carefully, 'you're a good-looking guy, and…there are women here who find you attractive. You don't need to be alone.'

I stare at him, shocked. I get what he's saying, but it's too personal. I'm not sleeping with any of them.

'Not my thing.' I shake my head quickly.

He watches me. 'Do you…prefer men? Of course, there are guys here who would be quite happy to…'

'No,' I interrupt him loudly. 'No, it's nothing like that. I just…' My mind is desperately seeking the right words. 'It's just… I have a girlfriend.'

'She's not here.'

I shake my head, no. That's not the point. 'I have a girlfriend,' I repeat.

Gil looks at me. I sense him gauging what to say. 'Okay, Dominic. Personally, I think sex is a great release, and this place can get pretty tense, and…I think you could be a lot happier than you are, but it's your choice.'

I want him to get up and go. He can't talk to me about these things; I don't want it. But he doesn't move.

'You remind me of me, sometimes,' he says, his voice very low, 'when I was your age.'

I don't believe that.

'When I was fourteen,' he continues, slowly, 'my sister died. And I was angry, really angry, for a long time.'

I wasn't expecting that. Now he has my attention. He doesn't sound like Gil anymore, not the leader of the Disciples, but someone more normal. He is still, a flicker of emotion moving behind his eyes.

'You're very angry, Dominic. I know, because I can see it, and I've felt that way myself. You feel your father's loss, and your life's not what it should be, and it's not right and it's not fair. You're so full of rage nobody can be your friend, and you can't let anyone close. I've been there and pushed the world away too.'

I can't speak; my throat's choked, full of confused emotions. Gil is peeling back my skin. I want him to leave, right now, before he says anymore. But another part of me wants him to stay. He's the only one who knows just how bad I feel.

'Maybe,' I mutter. 'Something like that.'

He nods. I watch him raise his glass to his lips and drink down the rest of his milk.

'Well, at least we understand each other.' He moves to leave.

'Gil.' I suddenly hear my voice. 'When did you stop being angry?'

He looks at me, a long, concentrated moment. 'A part of me has never stopped being angry, but I've learnt to channel it into something more creative, more just and fair.'

I look at him. I feel so confused. I've hated him for who he is and what he's done to me, and yet, he understands.

'I don't know if I can do that,' I confess.

'No,' he says. 'Right now, you don't know, but I do. You can, Dominic. You will.' He sounds encouraging, even kind. He turns around and I watch him leave the room.

I sit there a while. My mind floods with questions. How did his sister die? What happened? I didn't read anything in the press reports about it. Is it a secret he's carried deep inside? I think of my own sister, and then stop thinking. I can't let my imagination go there; it's unbearable territory. Instead, I get up quickly and go back to the loft. When I go in, Flint is sleeping soundly, but Charley's eyes are open. I sense she's been waiting on my return. I kneel down beside her and, without saying a word, we hug one another.

'*We always love each other, don't we, Dom?*' she whispers into my thoughts.

'*Yes,*' I reply.

'*I know things have been difficult for you, me being with Flint, but…we still love each other?*'

'*Always,*' I promise.

Then I move to my sleeping bag. I lie down and gaze through the dark. I think of Gil. I don't hate him anymore.

CHAPTER 25

'There is nothing Sanjay doesn't know about explosives.' Gil introduces us to a tall, thin Indian man. He's clean-shaven and well dressed; he looks incongruous next to the rest of the Disciples. Yet he arrived earlier. He is one of them.

We all sit in Gil's room, a select group of five: Tom, Sanjay, Gil, Charley and me. We are beginning to understand what is expected of us. There is an oil pipeline deep below the sea's surface. It is one of LifeStar Corporation's leading projects. They claim the materials used, and the processes involved in extracting the oil, guarantee an end to spills and leaks. The Disciples are going to prove otherwise. With the right amount of explosives, they intend to blow a hole through it.

'Sanjay used to work for the other side,' Tom says proudly, 'so he knows exactly what to do to make this blow-out look like an operational failure on LifeStar's account. With the two of you placing the explosives, nobody will see or know a thing.'

Charley and I sit there silent. We have not agreed to this; we never would.

'You're important,' Gil says, 'because you've no need for bulky breathing apparatus, and we'll train you to navigate with minimal light. You'll be nothing but a brief shadow in the water like a seal or marine mammal. They'll know nothing. And we'll be hacking into their computer system, and that's all they'll be looking at afterwards.' He smiles.

We are not going to get out of this. I wonder where their hackers are, but guess I'll never know. They'll use them to disrupt one thing while Charley and I are expected to plant explosives. We won't be safe behind a laptop.

'How big a hole are you going to blow in the pipeline?' I'm trying to judge the danger we're in.

'Big enough to send gallons of crude oil into the sea,' Tom says.

'I don't understand.' I turn to Gil, alarmed. 'That means you're going to cause the kind of environmental disaster you say you're always fighting against.'

Gil holds my gaze. 'Sometimes, it's necessary to make very difficult decisions. In this case, ultimately, the end will justify the means. This will be LifeStar Corporation's disaster. They'll be forced to explain themselves, they'll lose money on the stock market. They'll have to reconsider the project. Their exploitation of the natural world must stop.'

'*We cannot and will not do this.*' Charley's voice is loud in my head.

'*I know.*'

'Will we come back alive?' she challenges them. 'If you're going to blow a hole that big, it surely takes a lot of explosives.'

Gil and Tom grow still. I think they're angry; we're asking the wrong questions.

'The Disciples do not involve themselves in suicide missions,' Gil says clearly. 'Suicide bombers are fanatics who love death more than life. We have nothing to do with that. Tom is training you, and you are going to practice until you drop with exhaustion if necessary, to ensure you plant that bomb successfully and return *safely*,' he stresses.

'Sanjay is a professional,' Tom says coolly, 'and you will be professional. Have no doubt about it.'

'*We cannot and will not do this!*' Charley screams in my thoughts.

'Understand?' Gil checks, growing impatient.

'Yes.' I nod. 'We understand.'

We spend the afternoon listening to Sanjay, looking at diagrams and touching models of what we've got to work with. Tom is ever present. I can't fully comprehend that, in time, we're actually meant to plant a bomb. Something or someone will surely intervene to stop it? Maybe the security services will find us? That might be the best outcome.

'These three wires are essential to the device going off. The first wire will already be firmly in place.' Sanjay points to the model. 'But the second and third wire you'll need to insert once the bomb's in situ. The second goes in easily, but this third one,' he says, dangling it before us, 'is where it gets tricky.'

I'm finding it hard to concentrate; my mind is pushing it away.

'And when you're in the water,' Tom instructs, 'you're working virtually in the dark and it's cold. We'll keep taking you out on the sea. You've got to get used to it, and that needs to happen quickly.'

'You'll also practise here.' Gil walks through the door carrying a huge bucket of ice. 'We'll blindfold you and freeze your fingers to replicate the conditions.'

I look at the bucket. I realise the next few hours are going to be painful, let alone what follows. I promise myself I will be brave. I turn to Charley, but her thoughts are silent.

At some point, the pain of my hands freezing becomes too much. My eyes fill, and I pray the blindfold absorbs my tears.

'I don't mind you crying, Dominic.' I hear Gil's voice. 'You just have to get the wires in the device correctly.'

Charley is silent. She does what they want and she does it well.

She says nothing. Gil watches her closely. He'll sense our defiance. I know he will, and that's dangerous.

Two weeks later, Gil gives the evening lecture. The more they prepare us to plant that bomb, the more I hate him again. Yet when he speaks, he's brilliant. Despite myself, I can't stop watching him. His presence fills the room. He has unswerving conviction. Is that what makes him so strong and self-assured? He doesn't seem afraid of anything. Did my father feel that too when he prepared to release LifeStar's secrets? Did certainty make him brave?

The lecture ends. The group breaks up and most people go to the kitchen for refreshments. I stay seated and Gil walks over. It's the first time he's acknowledged me in days. His face is animated; he loved giving that lecture.

'What are you thinking?' he asks, his manner relaxed. He sits beside me.

'That you're good, Gil,' I reply honestly. 'When you speak, you're much better than the others. You've got something...' I search for the right word. There was something I read about him over and again. 'I can see why people call you charismatic.'

'How flattering of you.' He smiles at me. 'But...that doesn't change the fact that you don't believe what I say, do you?'

He speaks with such ease, his body relaxed, that I almost miss how dangerous his question is.

'Yes, I do,' I say carefully.

'Dominic, you don't lie very well.' There is a long pause between us. I hate the way he can see through me.

'I believe some of what you say,' I continue, growing nervous. 'It's what Dad said too about capitalism being riddled with inequalities, and that the system is destructive and corrupt. That's...all stuff I can see.'

'But…there are other things you have difficulty with?'

I scan the room looking for Charley and Flint, but they're not there. I can't get up and walk away. I have to answer. I decide on the truth.

'I think a lot of what you say is right. I can see it's true. The problem is…what you want to do about it. I don't believe in violence. Violent action is wrong and…what you want Charley and me to do is particularly wrong. The end does not justify the means.' I can't look at him. I've spoken the truth and now he'll punish me. I should have lied. I'm not playing the game like I should.

'Well,' he says softly, 'I've thought that way too.'

I turn to face him, surprised. There's nothing threatening about him. He's not angry. 'You're wrong,' he continues, looking relaxed. 'But I understand why you feel the way you do.'

'Do you?'

'Of course, Dominic. Nobody *wants* to take violent action. Not unless they're sadists. But sometimes…it's called for.' He sounds reasonable. 'Come, I want to show you something.'

He stands up and motions for me to follow. I leave the room with him.

CHAPTER 26

I walk with Gil to his study. The room is cold and we are alone. As he closes the door, I shiver. I need to be careful. He sits at the table and turns on his laptop. He motions for me to join him then brings up an image of an austere, concrete building. It's round in shape and looks like a fortress.

'This is where we now know they're holding your father. Colchester House or, as it's known in the trade, "the jelly mould".'

'The jelly mould?'

'Unfortunately, the truth of what they do in Colchester House is in the nickname. They'll be trying to mould your father into something else, someone more compliant.'

I look at the building and my stomach churns. Legs turn to jelly out of fear. I don't want to think of my father in pain.

Gil points to the building and what I think is a doorway. 'It has five entry and exit points, a range of security doors within, and it's very well guarded. At this point in time, we've no chance of breaching it.'

'Will you ever?' I ask. I don't want my father to spend another moment there.

'If we do,' Gil says slowly, 'it won't be the result of a peaceful protest. It will require force, significant force.' He turns to me. 'I don't like violent action either, Dominic. I long for the day we can give it up, but…this is their violence. Did your father speak to you about the kind of information he was trying to give us?'

I nod, yes.

'Weapons of mass destruction,' he says. 'What part of weapons of mass destruction isn't violent?' He watches me closely. 'Your father was a man of conscience, of *peace*,' he stresses, 'but this is what they're doing to him.' He motions to the screen. 'They're holding him under terrorist legislation, without trial, of course, because then the truth would come out. And they're subjecting him to…' He grimaces.

'Stop.' I don't want to hear this.

Gil is quiet. He knows I'm upset.

'How do we counter their violence,' he continues, 'if not through other violent means?'

The question hangs in the air.

'If we lived in a just world, Dominic, your father would have managed to give us the documents he wanted. We'd have leaked them to a national paper, and once verified and published, there would have been a public outcry, protests, questions asked in parliament, and the possibility of real democratic, non-violent change. But we don't live in a just world. The system doesn't work like that. Instead, your father's incarcerated. There's no trial date set. Editors are gagged and journalists can be threatened. The internet is a playground for political lies and fake news. Those in power protect their interests whatever the cost to individual, humble lives. Nothing is allowed to change, not through peaceful means.'

I look into his eyes; they are full of fire. I have no response. Everything he's said makes sense.

'How do we counter their violence, if we don't use violence back?' Gil won't let the question go.

'I don't know.'

'No, you don't. But your father came to us because, ultimately, he knew it would only be through force that he'd see freedom again. Nobody else is fighting for him but the Disciples. And it is only the

Disciples who are prepared to defend his children.'

Gil's eyes hold mine. He means every word he's said. I don't know how to argue back; my words are just a jumble in my head.

'Did you ever meet Dad?' I ask, because I need to know.

'Yes.' He nods.

'Where and when?'

'I only share information on a need-to-know basis, and you don't need to know that.'

'I do,' I push.

He smiles, benignly, like I'm a small child. I hate that; I'm not a child.

'I miss him,' I confess. 'I need you to tell me more.'

Gil grows still. He watches me closely. 'I'll tell you this,' he eventually continues. 'When we did meet, he told me he felt physical pain when he thought about the impact of his proposed actions on you and Charley. That what he regretted most about his mistakes was how they would affect you.'

It's just like Dad put in his letter.

'And…I told him,' Gil slows, 'that any decision he made was his, and his alone, to make. But either way, he would have to live with it for the rest of his life.'

I know deep down they met. What Gil is saying is true; my father said those things. He's a Disciple.

'Sometimes, we have to make difficult choices,' Gil says, his eyes on me.

I can't speak, not for a while. The air in the room feels heavy to breathe.

'Can I go now?' Everything hurts.

'You can go.'

I stand and turn to leave. I know I'm going to cry, but I won't do it in front of him.

'One more thing.' Gil stops me.

I swallow hard.

'Yes,' I say, turning to him.

'Tom's concerned you're not making enough effort in training.'

'What?' The conversation's turned. A pit of fear opens in my stomach.

'Charley's performing better than you, and given your height and build, your muscle strength in comparison to hers, it shouldn't be that way. Tom thinks you're holding back on us. And now... I can see you have been holding back on us.'

'No,' I protest.

Gil shakes his head, and motions for me to stay quiet.

'Tom's thought you lazy and disobedient, but I can see you've just not understood. Not what's really happening, or the war raging around you, or the part your father and the Disciples play.'

He stops. I hold my breath.

'The truth is painful,' he says, 'but I've explained enough now...and I expect your loyalty and obedience. See clearly, Dominic, and you'll realise there is hope on the horizon.'

I stand there. My lower lip starts to tremble. I can't respond.

'Go.' He dismisses me.

I leave his room. I rush to the bathroom and slam the door shut. I'm shaking.

CHAPTER 27

'I won't do it,' Charley says, fiercely. We are alone in the loft. 'I can't, Dom. I'm going to tell them I refuse.' She stands tall. 'Enough is enough. I don't know what they'll do to us. I'm afraid, of course, but I won't blow up that pipeline. I've discussed it with Flint. He's prepared to take the consequences with us.'

We have just spent an agonising night in the freezing sea. Tom was brutal. He told us that, ultimately, only one of us would carry out the operation. The other would stay behind. 'What kind of brother are you?' he whispered in my ear. He wanted me to push myself harder.

Now, Charley and I are meant to get some sleep. Flint is downstairs with the rest of the house. I'm too tired for this, but Charley means what she says.

'Charley, you can't refuse.' My conversation with Gil still reverberates in my head. 'We…we can't say no. It doesn't work like that.'

'I won't do it, Dom,' she insists.

'I don't think you get the situation. Gil will not let us refuse. You don't realise just how much Dad was one of them.' I've wanted to tell her that for days.

She pauses, unsure for a moment. 'Is that what he told you?' She looks upset. 'He can tell you that, Dom, but…we're not Dad, and I don't believe him anyway.'

I feel a strange kind of agony. I want her to understand the predicament we're in.

'I'm going to refuse Gil,' she says. 'I think we should go to him now, all of us, you, me and Flint, and we tell him we'll have nothing more to do with them.' She makes it sound easy.

I close my eyes. I'm so tired, but my sister is losing the plot. I've got to protect her before she gets herself hurt, really hurt.

'I will not blow up that pipeline,' she repeats as if I don't understand.

For a moment, my thoughts are frantic, desperately seeking a way through this. And then I have a flash of illumination: what Gil and Tom want; how I can protect Charley; how Flint and I survive too, because she can't say no.

'It's okay,' I say softly, opening my eyes. 'You don't have to. I'll get them to use me instead.'

She stops, still. 'No, Dom,' her voice shakes, 'you cannot blow up that pipeline either.'

We stand opposite each other; I feel slightly dizzy.

'*I want to protect you,*' I whisper into her mind.

'*And I want to protect you,*' she protests back.

I have to stay sharp. I have to find a way: a plan starts forming at the back of my head. '*I'll carry out the operation.*' It's important now we only speak through our thoughts. '*But…that doesn't mean I won't sabotage it.*'

She looks at me, shocked.

'*What would you do,*' I continue, '*if you wanted to mess it up, but make it look like you'd done your best?*'

Our eyes lock; I can see her beginning to understand.

'*The third wire?*'

I nod. '*They've made it clear it's the hardest to put in place, and without it, the device won't explode.*'

'*But we've also rehearsed it, endlessly.*'

'*We have, but that isn't doing it for real,*' I say, following my thoughts through, '*and in a live situation, there are things that can't always be planned for. I don't know, maybe I find something down there that's unexpected, or the darkness becomes too disorientating, or…I'll think of something.*'

I watch her expression. She's struggling to believe me, that it's possible.

'*I'll have tried my best,*' I tell her. '*I'll have done everything as instructed, as rehearsed, but in the end the bomb just doesn't explode, and it's not from lack of effort.*'

'*But then what will they do to you, Dom? If it doesn't blow up, they won't care why not, they'll just punish you.*'

'*Not if they believe I gave my all. I'm a loyal and obedient Disciple: I'm gutted I didn't succeed, I pushed myself to my limit, but somehow it went wrong. They'll have to forgive me. Even Gil must get things wrong sometimes.*'

Charley is quiet, taking in what I've said. 'I feel sick,' she says aloud. 'You can't do it. It's too dangerous.'

'*What? Sabotaging the operation or convincing them not to punish me?*'

'Both,' she retorts.

I shake my head, no. '*Refusing them is more dangerous.*'

She looks at me a long moment. I wait patiently. '*What if you fail?*' she says, finally considering it.

'*What? To leave out the necessary wire? Either of us could do that with ease.*'

'*But what if you can't convince them you're loyal and obedient? They'll kill you, Dom. I'd rather refuse them now, if that's the consequence – then at least we die without lying. At least we're true to who we are.*'

'*Nobody's going to die,*' I tell her. '*I've figured out enough about Gil and the Disciples to convince them. You couldn't do it, but I can.*'

Her eyes are full of anxiety. *'And I also know,'* she says, *'that Gil wants your soul. He takes you aside. He talks to you. But he doesn't do that with me or Flint. Why do you think that is?'* She pauses. *'Because he wants you, and he believes he can get you.'*

'No, Charley. You're wrong,' I protest.

'What if you fail…' she says slowly, *'because you really become one of them, loyal and obedient…a Disciple, like he's convinced you Dad was?'*

I shake my head, hurt. *'I can't believe you said that.'* I'm the one who's prepared to risk myself to protect her, to look after her. Dad told me to do that, but she doesn't understand.

Her eyes mist. *'That's my fear, Dom. As somebody who loves you and doesn't want to lose you. I'm afraid you'll become one of them.'*

That really upsets me, but I hide it. 'What you're afraid of will never happen,' I say aloud. 'I promise.'

CHAPTER 28

The days get shorter, the nights longer. It's October, a month I usually enjoy, but now, I'm increasingly nervous. I think they'll want to blow up that pipeline soon. Before it gets too cold and maybe before the clocks go back. I try to ask Tom about it, but he gives nothing away.

One evening, the bell rings announcing dinner. We go downstairs, but the communal dining area is in darkness. That's not normal. We stand still and silent, trying to figure out what's going on.

'Surprise!' A voice calls out.

The lights go up in the room. Everyone is there, and my eyes move to a large banner hanging on the back wall: 'Happy Birthday!'

'Oh, my God,' Charley says slowly.

'Happy birthday, sweetheart.' Baz comes forward to give Charley a hug. 'Time to party!' he says playfully.

We never told anyone when our birthday was, but now every Disciple is looking at us, relaxed and smiling. There are bottles of booze on the table (something I've not seen before), and a variety of party food laid out to eat. My eyes find Tom, and even he looks friendly.

Tom and I have not had the easiest time together, not since Gil told me about his concerns. I don't think he likes me. But we were out on the sea again last night, and I pushed myself hard. I swam ahead of Charley, as I do every time now, the gap between us widening. I know they have to pick me for the mission; I've got to be good, and much better than her. Tom pulled me back on board and I was gasping, winded with the effort.

'At last,' he muttered under his breath.

Now, he walks towards me. He wraps his arms around me in a hug. 'Happy birthday, Dominic.' His voice is no longer harsh. I embrace him back, which feels strange. I've never hugged any of them before. He smiles at me as we release each other.

'You're finally becoming a Disciple,' he says softly.

I feel myself blush, but it's a small triumph.

'I guess,' I reply. 'And…' I look round at the party they've laid on. 'This is great. Can I…can I have a beer?'

'Of course.' He almost laughs. 'It's there for all of us.'

I let myself relax. I figure I'm only seventeen once, and if for one night I can live without fear and anxiety then I will. I drink and eat and dance. Charley and Flint let go too, but they're much better dancers than me. At some point, I look around for Gil. He's leaning against a doorway, quietly watching us all.

'Gil,' I say, sauntering over, 'aren't you going to join in?' I raise my bottle of beer, aware he's empty handed.

'There's a strict rule that whenever we party, two people stay sober and on guard. Tonight, I'm one of the two.' Still, he smiles at me. 'Happy birthday, Dominic.'

'Thanks, and…I do feel happy,' I admit, a little drunk. 'We should party more often.'

'That would be good,' he replies. 'One day, when the world's a better place, we'll party for days at a time.'

'Yeah, that would be good. And I'd like to see you drink, Gil. I can't imagine what you're like when you're drunk.'

'No?' He chuckles.

'No…but then again, I can't imagine you ever letting go.'

I realise I should probably shut up. I'm best not talking too much to Gil.

He looks at me, amused. 'I can let go,' he assures me, but something in the way he says it makes me think of sex. I don't doubt he's had lots of it. And suddenly, I miss Mary.

'This would be perfect,' I say, taking a chance, 'if Mary was here. If that could happen, if Gregory's daughter could be here, it would be perfect.' I'm glad for the alcohol. It means I've the guts to say such things.

'You really love her, don't you?'

'Yeah. She knows me. That's what matters. Deep down, she knows who I am.'

He keeps smiling. 'Well…we'll see what we can do. Next time.'

I realise he means it; I hear it in his voice.

'I'm glad you get it,' I tell him, because he does understand.

'Sometimes, Dominic, I know you too.'

'Maybe you do,' I acknowledge, and then we're both smiling at each other.

Gemma saunters over. 'Come dance with me, Gil.' She is the prettiest woman there; of all the Disciples, she's the most beautiful in my eyes, but also Gil's. I've realised for some time they're boyfriend and girlfriend, if that's what you can ever call Disciples. She smiles at him, her lips stained with red wine.

'Dance with the birthday boy,' he says, motioning to me. She looks momentarily disappointed then turns and takes my hand. I decide to go with her; so what if she'd rather be with Gil? Tonight she can dance with me.

Later, the party changes gear. The music slows, and soft romantic songs play out of the sound system. People slouch around on cushions and chairs. They seem to melt into each other, couples kissing, hands exploring, it's all getting intimate. Flint and Charley are giggling and kissing in a corner. I lean my head back on the sofa and shut my eyes. The world spins slightly behind them. I've enjoyed myself and I don't want to feel alone, but if I stay here long enough I will now.

Someone taps my shoulder. I open my eyes.

'Shall we get out of here?' It's Gil.

'Out of here?' I sit up. 'I didn't think anybody got out of here, house rules.'

'Sometimes they do,' he says matter-of-factly. 'There's somewhere I'd like to take you.'

I look at him, bemused. I've never been allowed out of the place except under guard, and only for operational purposes.

'Alright,' I say, although I've no idea what's going on.

He motions for me to follow him out of the room. I glance back briefly at Charley and Flint; they're too engrossed with each other to notice me.

Gil takes me outside. It's pitch black. He passes me a head torch and puts one on himself. We walk round the mansion and approach what I'd always thought was a deserted outhouse. He pulls back one of the double doors and switches on the light. For the first time, I see it's a huge garage.

'Wow.' I'm dumbstruck. I'm looking at a row of vintage cars. They're in pristine condition: the bodywork, the paint, the polished chrome. There is the smell of petrol and leather, even cigarette smoke. I inhale deeply. This place is amazing. We walk past the cars to the back of the building.

'I can't believe this,' I say, stopping at an Aston Martin that must be sixty, seventy years old. It's beautiful.

'They're great, aren't they?' Gil comments. 'But we don't get to touch them. It's part of the agreement that allows us to be here.'

Gil opens a door at the back of the garage. It leads into a small workroom. Various tools and mechanical parts line the shelves. In the middle of the floor is an old worn-out motorbike. I guess it too must be sixty or seventy years old.

'Norton.' I read the name on the black painted metalwork.

'This is my baby,' Gil says, bending down to stroke it. 'Don't be put off by the bodywork, she still goes.' He glances over at me. 'Ever been on a motorbike before?'

'No.' I shake my head, but smile.

'Up for it?' I think he's going to drive fast.

'I'm up for it,' I tell him.

There are two worn leather jackets hanging on the wall. He puts one on and passes me the other. I zip it up, but it's still too big. He walks the bike outside. It doesn't look like it will hold together. Still, he throws his leg over it, and indicates I get on behind.

'What about helmets?' I say, aware I can see nothing ahead.

'This isn't about feeling safe, Dominic,' he tells me. 'But don't worry, you won't come off.' He starts the engine. 'You'll need to hold on tight.'

I'm unsure where to put my hands, and gently grip the sides of his jacket.

'You'll have to hold me a lot tighter than that,' he advises.

He revs the engine, and then we're racing forward. We charge down the driveway and out into the open countryside. I have no hope of looking cool as I hug him quickly, my embrace tight, because it's the only way to stay on. Darkness spreads out on either side; there is only limited light from the front of the bike. Gil cannot see where we're going, and the road beneath is nothing but skidding earth, stone and ditch. We bounce up and dip down – I'm not sure how we stay on. Gil should slow down to match the conditions but instead he accelerates. The tyres slip and slide. I realise I'm finding it difficult to breathe, clutching his jacket, trying to stay on. Adrenalin courses through me.

Suddenly, we hit something hard. The bike takes off – we're almost flying. Gil somehow keeps it upright on landing. My eyes and ears are acutely alert to danger. My bones rattle. Mud sputters up. It plasters my jeans, cold and wet. Then I sense we're on an incline, moving up to higher ground.

'Shit!' Gil exclaims.

Light bounces off a tree ahead. We're too close; we're going to hit it. Gil swerves to avoid crashing into it, and then we're going over. I can feel my hands slipping away from him. I anticipate the ground slashing my skin. But Gil's leg smacks the earth, and he forces us back into position. I'm breathing too quickly, my hands shaking. I want to tell him to slow down or stop, but I can't find my voice. I think it's possible he'll kill us, kill us both.

At last, we reach a clearing at the top of a hill. Gil brings the bike to a halt. We are both breathing hard. I can feel the sweat on my body despite the cold. I'm charged with adrenalin. I release my embrace of his body. I want to speak, but still, words won't come.

'That was exhilarating.' He exhales.

My teeth are chattering. 'You could've killed us, Gil,' I manage to say. 'You're reckless. Shit, you are scary.'

He laughs. 'Come on, Dominic, don't you feel alive? You're seventeen. Don't you want to feel this alive?'

I don't reply. He slowly gets off the bike. I wait until I can breathe more easily, before I get off and stand by him. We're quiet. My eyes slowly adjust to the dark terrain and the sky above.

'Sometimes,' he says softly, 'I like to come here. When I need to be on my own.'

The light on the motorbike is still on, the engine ticking over.

I can see his outline and the look on his face. He's calm now, almost pensive. He gazes out and up at the sky.

'See that line of stars.' He points into the distance. 'Follow it and you're looking at the plough.'

I try to trace the sparks of light. 'I'm not sure what I'm looking at,' I confess. 'I've never really got astronomy.'

He comes closer, puts his arm around my shoulder and guides me where to look, slightly to the left. 'See it now?'

I follow his lead. 'Yeah, I do now.'

He turns to me and smiles. I look back out at the stars. There are more there than I'd thought possible. The sky is endless, the moon far away. Suddenly, I'm flooded with the most positive feeling. It flushes through my veins. I'd felt such fear on the journey, but now there's a kind of bliss; I know everything in the world is as it should be. I feel it on the deepest level. I'm part of this vast, starlit universe, beautiful and infinite. I do not need to be afraid. Finally, there is no fear. And Gil's presence is good, standing next to me; it's as it should be. We are both a part of this. We belong to something bigger than ourselves.

Our eyes meet. His face is still. He looks like Jesus, serious and calm. I know now how special he is. He has a quality I can't describe, although I feel it tonight. He can see beneath the surface of things, of me and the world, to a deeper truth. I believe it's why my father went to him. It's what makes him Kingfisher. Charley and Flint will never understand, but they don't know him like I do.

'Ready to go back?' he asks.

'No.' I shake my head. 'I'm not sure I ever want to go back.'

We don't leave immediately. I'm glad, at least, we stay a while longer.

I go into the piano room. I'd been avoiding it, but now it's the most natural place to go. Elsewhere in the house, the party's breaking up. Gil slunk off with Gemma when we got back. I sit on the piano stool, lift the instrument's lid and gaze at the white and black keys. I stretch and wriggle my fingers in preparation. I play a few scales, my fingers moving up and down. Some in the major key, minor key and blues. I'm impressed; the piano sounds good. I didn't expect it to be in tune.

I close my eyes and feel it rising up inside. Music. A piece of Bach, one I've always loved, even if it's classical. It moves smoothly, repetitively up the key. A rising tide of beautiful sound. I hear it in my head, and then my fingers follow on the keys.

CHAPTER 29

It's evening. Charley and I go to Gil's study where Tom wants to speak to us alone. It's been days since the party, and the mood now is very sober. We stand before him.

'The assignment you've been preparing for we're calling Operation Gideon,' Tom says, serious, 'after the biblical warrior, because that's what you become now. Warriors.'

He watches us closely. I calculate it must be happening soon, which means an end to all the training.

'As I've told you, strategically, as well as practically, it makes sense to involve only one of you in this operation.'

My heart quickens, but I need to stay calm.

'The question is…' he says slowly, 'which of you do we use?'

My sister's body stiffens. If Tom says the wrong thing, Charley will crack. They have to pick me; I've worked hard for this. I must be their choice.

'There are two qualities essential for our success: physical stamina and nerve,' he continues. 'For a long time, Dominic, your stamina concerned us, but you've improved. You're stronger than Charley now, as we would expect. However, the second quality, nerve, is sometimes harder to judge.'

I sense my sister's rising defiance, but she must keep her mouth shut.

'You've got a quality, Charley, we like. And sometimes women can display an incredible ruthlessness when carrying out assignments.' The tension in the room is palpable. He's pushing her. I need to say something.

'And me?' I ask.

'And you…' Tom says, his eyes narrowing on me. 'Gil insists, Dominic, that he wants you to carry out this operation.'

He's been talking as though they hadn't decided which of us to use, but now it's clear they had. He's been playing with us, a cruel game.

'Gil's made the right decision.' I manage to hold my voice steady. My heart is pounding, but this is a triumph. I don't think I'd have been Tom's choice. 'Or don't you agree?' I dare to challenge him.

Tom almost smiles. 'In this particular instance, Gil's convinced me. It's possible next time we'll agree on Charley.'

'*There will be no next time,*' Charley hisses into my head, seething.

'You can go now, Charley.' It's Gil, behind us. I didn't hear him approach. He walks into the room. 'We need to speak to Dominic alone.'

I watch my sister's face pale. She doesn't move; something is wrong. 'If you kill my brother, Gil,' she explodes, full of rage. 'I will kill you!'

'*No, Charley,*' I yell into her thoughts.

Gil is very still. Then he strikes her hard across the face. I hear my sister's cheek scrunch. She screams. Tears spring to her eyes; her lips tremble.

'You will never speak to me like that again,' Gil says.

Charley's shaking and so am I. I can't believe he hit her, and with such force. It takes everything in my power not to hit him back. He should never have done that. Gil's eyes turn on me, watching my response closely. I swallow hard. Whatever happens next, I cannot let the situation escalate.

'Charley,' I say, but it's difficult to speak. I feel quite sick. 'You should go.' It's what they told her to do. She needs to leave, to find Flint, to calm down. Flint knows there is no escape, and I'm the only one who can carry this off.

She turns to Gil. Her eyes spark with defiance, but she's also afraid.

'You're very beautiful, Charley,' he continues gently. 'Let's keep it that way.'

His threat turns my stomach. I don't want to believe he'd hurt her more; he just wants to squash her disobedience.

'Go,' he insists. 'We need to speak to Dominic.'

She turns to me and shakes her head. '*We should have defied them, Dom. Both of us. That was the only thing to do.*'

It's the most terrible moment. I realise she doesn't believe in me. She thinks I'm one of them; I'm going to blow up that pipeline. She leaves the room. I feel an emptiness inside that widens in my chest; it's hard to breathe. I am glad there are a few moments of silence.

Gil eventually speaks. 'I admire your self-control.'

'Do you?' I mumble, aware I'm so upset I don't know if I can hide it.

'I do,' he replies. 'That was hard for you to witness, but you controlled yourself because you know better.'

'Do you always have to see through me?'

'As it happens, I can see through Charley and Flint too.' I feel such menace emanating from him. He knows our defiance. 'I do not expect you to fail, Dominic, that's why we chose you.'

Suddenly, everything I thought possible is unravelling. What in the world made me think I could bluff blowing up a pipeline? I'm like a small, ridiculous child. One who thinks they can play with fire without getting burnt. Charley's gone and I am alone.

'It happens tomorrow night,' Tom says matter-of-factly.

'What?' I didn't think it would be that soon.

'We decided not to tell you earlier,' Tom continues, 'because it's your first active operation. You're bound to be nervous. We don't want you to feel that for any length of time. It's never useful.'

'Okay,' I say, aware I have to stay sharp.

'You'll go out on the boat with Tom and Baz,' Gil instructs, 'just like you have those other times. Gemma and I will be waiting in the truck at the coast. While we're with you, we'll be armed. We can protect you should anything kick off. But once in the water, you'll be on your own.'

He pauses. I take in what he's said.

'Should anything kick off?' I query, aware nobody's spoken like this before.

'We're armed, because although we've not mentioned it before, that part of the coastline is searched periodically by LifeStar Corporation's security guards.'

This is all new information. 'And are they armed?' I ask, my fear increasing.

Gil nods, yes. 'They are.'

I try not to stutter. 'So…you're saying…that…Operation Gideon is more dangerous than you told me?'

'It was always going to be dangerous,' Tom responds. 'That's why I've spent so long training you.'

'What about their computer system – you said you'd disrupt it?' I remind them.

'Yes,' Tom replies, 'but that won't disarm those guards.'

I stare into both their faces; they're hiding nothing now.

'Can I speak to you alone, Gil?' I ask.

He nods at Tom, who leaves the room.

'I'd like to ask you,' I say slowly, 'as the man behind this operation, as leader of the Disciples. As someone I hope tells me the truth…am I going to die tomorrow?' He won't like the question, but I have a right to know.

'You're not going to die tomorrow.'

'How do you know?' I challenge him.

'Because there is something you're failing to acknowledge,' Gil answers. 'The Disciples are absolutely and completely loyal and committed to each other. We act together because individual failure is not an option – it becomes collective failure.' He pauses, but only for a moment. 'You will not die tomorrow,' he states clearly. 'Tom, Baz, Gemma and I are not going to allow that to happen because it would mean we'd all be facing significant harm…and that is not going to happen.'

I don't see how his words add up, but I need to believe him, otherwise I do not know how I survive. I never wanted to be a warrior.

'That's my commitment to you, Dominic. As a Disciple,' he says pointedly. 'While on a more personal level,' he softens, 'there's something unique about you, and I have no intention of losing you.'

His gaze alters, it's as though he's a friend.

'I'm afraid,' I admit.

'Of course,' Gil acknowledges, and not unkindly. 'It's a perfectly natural response. Fear, to a point, is a good thing when it keeps the adrenalin flowing, when it ensures you stay sharp and alert. It protects you. But get too scared and you risk messing up. We'll all be afraid tomorrow, but just to the right degree.'

'And what stops you getting too afraid?'

'Knowing that you're part of a team. You're not out there alone. The four other people involved with you are completely behind you, as you must be for them. We work as one, and nothing is more powerful than that. That's what keeps fear in check. We have a mission, we will not be beaten.'

I'm silent. There is no way out of this.

'One day, Dominic, you will see your father again,' Gil promises. 'This violence will come to an end. We will live in a free and just society.' His eyes hold mine. 'Isn't that what you want?'

My mind fills with darkness, like a loch at midnight, and I feel myself drowning. I will have to be a Disciple for my own safety, for any of us to get out of this alive.

'That's what I want,' I reply.

'You've got a big day tomorrow,' Gil says gently. 'Go up to the loft now.'

Does he imagine I'll be able to sleep?

'There's someone waiting there for you.' He smiles.

CHAPTER 30

I leave Gil's room. My heart is racing. Nothing feels real anymore. Tomorrow, I'm expected to plant a bomb, and tonight…I go up the stairs. Dare I believe what he just said is true? I reach the loft and gently push the door open. Mary is standing there, silent and still. Gil's done it – he's let me see her again. Sweet, beautiful Mary. She turns to me and for a few long moments we stare at each other. Then I'm running to her, and she to me. We embrace.

'Mary, Mary.' I squeeze her tight.

She holds me and she's crying. We kiss and hug. I don't want to let her go, not now we're together again, but gradually we grow calmer. We sit side by side on the floor.

'I've been so afraid for you,' she tells me. 'I cried every day after you'd gone. I couldn't believe my father betrayed you.'

'No,' I say, 'but you didn't.'

She looks at me with watery eyes; I sense how lonely she's been. 'Dad told me to stop crying, it was pointless, the police were coming for you, and it was better you were with the Disciples than them.'

I'm quiet. I no longer know what would have been better. 'It's been very hard here,' I admit, 'but I'm okay.' I don't say more than that. She can't know what I'm expected to do.

'I've missed you,' she says. 'I didn't know it could hurt so much. And then…' She stalls. 'Then I got scared…my period didn't come.'

My breath solidifies in my throat. We had unprotected sex. I didn't think twice about it then, but I am now.

'I thought, I don't know what I'm going to do if I'm pregnant,' she continues, 'how Dad would react.'

I'm silent. I don't want to admit how sick I feel.

'But it was just late. Two weeks late. I think because of all the upset at what happened.' Her face clouds with sadness.

I close my eyes and swallow the bile rising in my throat. 'I'm sorry, Mary.'

'If I had been pregnant with your baby, I would have kept it.'

She's letting me know she loves me, but I can't respond. I don't know how I'd have reacted to being a father, but doubt I would have been great.

'I've not been very good for you, have I, Mary?'

'I've had moments,' she says, looking in my eyes, 'when I have thought I should have stayed away from you, like you warned me. But…really…I think you have been good for me. Even if it's hurt, it's been a good kind of pain.'

'Is there such a thing as a good kind of pain?' I ask.

'Yes,' she says, nodding her head. 'The hurt you feel when you love someone and then they're not there. That's a good pain, in a way, because it lets you know you cared. It lets you know you loved them.'

Suddenly, I can't bear to continue the conversation. I cry and she kisses my tears. We kiss some more and then start to wriggle out of our clothes. I stop. I can't make any mistakes this time. I leave the room and move quickly to the bathroom. Fortunately, it's empty. There is a box of condoms in the cabinet. I retrieve a few and go back to the loft. She giggles as I tear open the wrapper and roll one down over me. We snuggle together in my sleeping bag but it's too small. Laughing, we undo the zip and throw a blanket over ourselves.

I don't know when Charley and Flint will return, but for now we're on our own. I kiss her and I love her. Nothing else matters.

At some point we wake, our bodies entwined. I'm aware we're still alone. Charley and Flint must be elsewhere. I think that's kind of them, giving us our privacy; maybe Gil arranged that too. Mary and I both know this may be the last time we see each other. We have sex again. I touch her in places I never imagined touching, we explore each other, we don't stop. I lose myself with her. I don't know how much longer I'll be alive, so what we do together is powerful and intense. I want it to last forever.

'Mary,' I ask her, when we're finally still. 'Will you remember me? Always?'

'Of course,' she whispers back. 'How could I forget you? You're the first person I've slept with, nobody forgets that.'

'But…will you remember me for more than sex?'

I realise if I become a Disciple tomorrow, the person she is with now will still die; I'll not be the same again. I want her to remember me as good, before things happen I can never take back.

She grows quiet. 'Of course, Dominic.' She holds me close. 'Sex is the way our bodies speak, but our souls talk too.'

I bury my head in her shoulder. I can't answer. I don't know what I wanted to hear, but it was something like that. Only she could say something like that.

'Thank you.' I move my lips against her skin. I know she'll understand. 'You're the best thing that's ever happened to me.'

I wake in the morning, my head buried in my pillow. Mary has gone. For a moment I wonder if I dreamed her, but my body quickly tells me otherwise. But of course, they wouldn't let her stay long. I turn my head slowly and see Tom standing near me. I've no idea how long he's been there.

'Dominic, you've got ten minutes to get up and down to Gil's study.' There is nothing hostile about him today.

I gaze round the room. The loft is suffused with light. Charley and Flint are not there; their beds have not been slept in.

'What time is it?' I ask.

'Eleven thirty. We let you sleep in, because you won't be sleeping tonight.'

I want to ask him when Mary went, but there's no point.

'Don't worry if you still feel tired,' he continues. I must look groggy. 'We'll give you something later to keep you awake.'

I let that sink in. 'You mean…drugs?'

'Amphetamines. We'll all be taking them,' he says with ease. 'Standard procedure, especially if we're working through the night.'

Neither Charley nor I were ever given them before, even though we swam at night. Everything is changing and changing fast. I wonder what I'm meant to do now. Most importantly, I've got to find Charley and Flint. I have to see my sister again after last night.

'I've got ten minutes?' I check.

'Ten minutes,' he confirms. 'Time to shower and get dressed.'

'I need to see Charley and Flint.'

'Forget it. They're in the gym working out. There's no time. Once you're in Gil's room, you don't come out until we go to the coast.'

I pause, stunned. 'No, I need to see them.'

'You will.' Tom smiles. 'Tomorrow morning, when we get back. Mission accomplished.'

CHAPTER 31

I get in the shower. I've got very little time. I don't get to say goodbye to Charley or Flint. That's not right, that can never be right, and Charley was upset yesterday. I'm trying to understand what's happening. I thought my night with Mary was a gift, something Gil had given me, but I can see it also kept me away from them. He knows their defiance. But now, I have to focus on the day ahead and, more importantly, the night ahead. Once I enter Gil's room, I can't predict what will happen.

I step out of the shower and suddenly Flint is there. He moves his hand to cover my mouth. 'They don't know I'm here,' he whispers, 'and you have to hear what I've got to say, and you need to shut up, 'cause there's very little time.'

Our eyes meet; I'm relieved to see him, but his are full of concern.

'I know Gil's got to you,' he continues. I move my lips to answer back, to argue no, but he just presses his fingers against them harder. 'I don't blame you, Dom. Okay, I'm letting you know, I don't blame you. That guy's worked hard on you. He's been grooming you from the start, and if he'd paid me that much attention, I might have fallen for him too, I probably would have. But he's got you, big time. I see it in the way you look at him, and in the way he behaves towards you.'

He stops. My thoughts blur with confusion. My eyes fill. The word 'grooming' reverberates round my head. What's Flint saying?

'Charley's in pieces,' he says, and I can see he's upset too. 'She thinks you're going to blow up that pipeline.'

Now, I'm struggling. I can't speak, not because Flint's hands across my mouth, but because my throat's too tight.

'And I...' His voice shakes. 'I don't know what you're going to do, but there's something I need you to know. I've figured out Kingfisher.' The word hangs in the air. He lowers his hand.

I'm silent; I need to hear this.

'I've figured it out, Dom, and you need to know before you plant that bomb: Gil is not Kingfisher. He never was. Kingfisher has always been about you. You and Charley.'

I feel light-headed. I hope I can take what he's going to say.

'The only person your dad knew you'd see for sure, after the police got him, was Rena,' Flint continues, his voice urgent. 'So the answer lies with Rena. Your dad left you a letter, and he told you to run. He said nothing about the Disciples, 'cause he didn't want you involved with them. They were never going to protect you. I don't care what Gil's made you believe.' Flint pauses. I've never heard him speak like this, so determined and intense.

'After your dad left his letter with Mum, I reckon he got scared – he really understood what his actions would do to you. It cut him up so bad he wrote you that final message, Kingfisher. It was too late for anything else.'

I imagine my father slipping that piece of paper into Charley's rabbit. I think of the pressure he must have been under. Maybe MI5 were banging at the door?

'You've always thought Kingfisher a person.' Flint shakes his head. 'That's never made sense – he'd have put it in his letter. He's telling you something else, Dom. Mum told me you asked her about Kingfisher, and what happened in her childhood. The day she and your dad argued about what a kingfisher was. And the answer is there, you just didn't see it. Me neither, not until now.' He stops, he's breathing hard.

'Mum's more special than you know,' he says softly. 'And in the end, your dad got that. When they were kids she saw a blue spirit, and your dad just saw a bird in a book, but that said everything about them.' He's shaking slightly. I sense how much he's wrestled with this, and how much he loves his mother, yet we've never really spoken about her.

'My mum's made mistakes,' Flint continues. 'She's no saint, but she's always lived by her heart, with love and imagination. She had the guts to keep me and stay strong even though Frank had died. She had the guts to ask your dad for money even though it hurt her, because, deep down, my mum cares.' He swallows. 'She always finds a way to see something good, or beautiful, like she saw that blue spirit. But your dad...the scientist, the smart one, the one who always got it right, he let rip at Rena sometimes. He never had any problem telling her when she was wrong.' Flint pauses, visibly upset. 'They didn't see each other for years, because she couldn't take the way he behaved. He put her down. And...my mum didn't have the heart to tell you that. She told you he'd been good, supporting her, but she hid from you what a shit he'd been too.'

Flint stops. I'm trying to take this all in, things I didn't know.

''Cause in the end...' Flint says, 'everything your dad stood for meant the only person he could trust was her.' His eyes fill. 'Your father loved you. I know it from what you've told me, and Charley. He loved you. But he messed up too, big time. Kingfisher is telling you how he wants you to live, and it's not about being like him. Don't make his mistakes. He wants you to live so when you see a kingfisher, you see a blue spirit. There is spirit in the world, Dom. In you and me and Charley. He wants you to see it, 'cause he couldn't, not until it was too late. That's why he sent you to Rena.'

We stand opposite each other, both close to tears. Everything I thought I knew, I thought I understood, is turned on its head. And I feel a terrible sadness. I didn't thank Rena for all she did. She was protective and kind, she took a risk taking us in, and all I did was judge her for the food she cooked and the state of her home. I didn't think she had anything much to say, probably like my father once did too. And Flint, he loves me more than I ever chose to realise.

'Come back safe,' he whispers.

We embrace. I can't speak, everything has gone beyond words; I'm crying. I just hold him tight and hope he knows. Hope he can feel what I can't say. I love him and I'm sorry. I got so much wrong.

'What the fuck is taking you so long?' Tom barges into the bathroom. 'Oh, shit,' he says on seeing Flint with me. We release our embrace.

'It's okay,' Flint says, sounding more normal. 'I'm gone.' He leaves the bathroom quickly.

Tom comes towards me. I flinch – I think he's going to hit me. But instead, he moves his hands to wipe my cheeks dry. Although his fingers are gentle, it feels the most menacing thing he's ever done.

'This is exactly why we didn't want you to see each other,' he says softly.

They did intentionally keep us apart.

'When you enter Gil's room,' he continues, 'you're a warrior. And warriors don't cry.' He takes a step back. 'Understand?'

I finally find my voice. 'I understand.'

CHAPTER 32

I sit in Gil's study. Flint's words turn in my head, but I can't think about them now. I have to concentrate. This is the most dangerous day of my life. There are more people in Gil's room than I've seen before. Sanjay is back with a few colleagues. Baz, Tom and Gemma are present, but Gil's also brought in Spike. Apparently, he's good with a gun.

I listen as they go through everything in detail: each action we'll take, intended outcome, and contingency plans if anything goes wrong. Far more effort has gone into Operation Gideon than I'd realised. They've been plotting the tides and weather, charting the movement of LifeStar Corporation's guards, and tracing every detail of the landscape and sea. The boat and truck we'll use have been serviced and fuelled.

But the Disciples do not have the capacity to bring down LifeStar Corporation's computer network. I'd always thought that an audacious plan. I'd liked it, because it meant what I'd do might diminish in importance. Yet now, the most that can happen is some local disruption and only for a few hours. Sanjay gives a technical explanation as to why. LifeStar have altered their system, increasing its resilience, and his colleagues would need more time to inflict the desired damage.

Gil takes in what he's said. He's not happy, and my mind grasps at hope. Maybe they'll call the operation off or delay it?

'We inflict as much damage as we can,' Gil instructs Sanjay.

'We go ahead. The blow-out is the most important thing.'

I am not going to get out of this. Gil focuses his attention on me.

'What did Flint say to you this morning?' The question drops lightly from his lips. Yet I know how careful I need to be.

'He…he just wanted to wish me luck.'

'If seeing him in any way impedes your performance,' Gil says without emotion, 'Flint will be punished for his actions. I don't have time to deal with him today, but I will.'

'He loves me, Gil.' It feels the wrong place to be saying such a thing, but I won't let him threaten Flint. 'He wants me to come back safely. Just like you do.'

Gil doesn't look convinced. 'We've got a lot of work to do.' He turns back to the group.

At some point, food is brought into the room. I hadn't realised how the hours had passed. We set off soon. We need to eat now to let it digest before we go. It's only when I raise my fork to my lips, I realise I'm shaking. That's not good. I try to hold my hand steady, but decide not to eat. I feel sick anyway.

Gil takes me aside. I sense the others in the room watching, although they at least pretend not to.

'If you can't eat,' Gil says softly, 'then you take some energy tablets before we go, and you keep them with you while you're swimming.' His manner is one of friendly concern.

'I can't eat.'

'You've got a long way to swim. Try and eat something if you can.' He produces a couple of pills from his pocket; they're small, in a plastic bag. He takes one out. 'This sort of thing always works best with food in your stomach.'

He holds the tablet out to me. Suddenly, I know I need to refuse him, to tell him I can't do it. I'll disobey.

'You can and will do this, Dominic,' he whispers. Why does he always know what I'm thinking? I swallow hard. Refuse, I tell myself.

'Fear is just an emotion,' he continues, 'and we are all capable of rising above our emotions.'

I look at him. He never doubts himself. He's never weak.

'I'm not as brave as you.' It's the only way I can put into words what I'm feeling. I can't refuse him, because I don't have the guts. I can't refuse him, because the punishment will be too great for all of us.

'You're brave,' he insists. 'I would never have picked you if I didn't know you were brave enough.'

What if, despite everything, Gil has got this right? This mission is possible, and it can change the world for the better? What if he can see something in me I can't see in myself? I can do this and survive.

'Trust me,' he says. His lips barely move. For a horrible moment, I think he's managed to speak into my mind.

I take the pill from him. He smiles.

We leave once it's dark. I'm wearing a wetsuit without fluorescent markings, and dark grease on my face. The others are in khaki or black, their faces also smeared for camouflage. We all shift outside and into the truck. Nobody speaks. The vehicle weaves its way down to the coast. I don't have a sense of time anymore, I'm just acutely alert. Every sound seems disproportionately loud; my eyes seek out any light in the dark.

We stop at a place on the coast I've never been before. Tom looks at his watch; he knows LifeStar's guards' routine.

'We've got twenty minutes,' he whispers. Twenty minutes to get on the water and away. We disembark quickly. Gil, Gemma and Spike keep guard. Tom, Baz and I go down to the sea. We take the inflatable boat with us. We clamber in and move off quickly, paddling almost soundlessly away.

The water is calm. We are silent. There is nothing to say – we know what we've got to do. The boat stops. Tom takes the device, carefully wrapped, and straps it to my back.

'Good luck,' he whispers as I slip overboard. I go under the water and quickly swim off.

The sea is dark and freezing. There is nothing but the sound and bubble of my own breath, and my arms and legs pushing through the water. The only light comes from the illuminated compass watch strapped to my left wrist. I go onto automatic pilot. We've rehearsed this many times, and I've got a distance to swim. Everything is quiet; that's what feels eerie, because in a matter of hours a bomb could explode, letting oil flood out. There will be no quiet then. I don't feel afraid – that surprises me too.

My mind is blank until Flint's words slowly seep into my thoughts. Everything he said about Kingfisher might be true. 'I know Gil's got to you…he's been grooming you from the start.' Flint said that too. He used the word *grooming*, but that doesn't relate to me. I'm not naïve, and Gil's not a paedophile.

'Terrorists groom people too,' Flint insists in my imagination.

'No!' I tell him. 'Not me.'

I remember Gil the night of my birthday. How we stood watching the stars, the light in the dark. 'He's an amazing person,' I admit to myself. 'He terrifies me, but he's strong and fearless. He knows what he wants and what he needs to do. That's more than I manage.'

I keep swimming and try not to think anymore. Eventually, I sense the pipeline ahead. Most of it is below the seabed, but at a few strategic points it surfaces. I've reached one of them. I see a slight alteration in the shading of the dark water. I'm there. I feel my heart pounding as I remove the bomb from my back. My hands are shaking. I gently put it in place. I pause. I feel sick. I push in the second wire. I touch the third. Now, I'm paralysed. I close my eyes. What do I do?

'You can and will do this, Dominic.' Gil's voice is clear in my head.

'Kingfisher is telling you how he wants you to live, and it's not about being like him.' Flint's voice is equally clear.

'Dad!' My thoughts scream. 'Tell me, guide me. What do I do?'

There is no answer. Nothing. I wait. I think of waiting forever. Maybe that's how I survive this? I never make the decision. I never leave the water. I die a different death.

'I know the colour of your soul.' It's Mary's soft, distinctive voice in my memory. 'It's blue, not a dark blue, a bright one, an azure blue, like…like the blue on a kingfisher.'

Suddenly, there is calm. I open my eyes again. I let go of the third wire. I know the answer. I hear them all, but I make the decision alone. I make it with my heart. Dad would want that. I turn around to swim away. Gil will probably kill me when the bomb doesn't explode. I will weep real tears before him, I will beg his forgiveness, but I will not wire that device. Then Gil can do to me what he chooses, but this is my choice.

I swim quickly away. I've taken too much time already. When I reach the boat, I'm breathless. They haul me over its edge and Tom motions to his watch.

'What the hell happened? You took longer than we planned.' His voice is pinched. 'Now we've less time to get to shore before it blows up.'

I don't respond, exhausted. They row hard. We reach the shore and Spike indicates it's all clear. We clamber up and back towards the truck. My body is weak now. My legs stiff. It's hard to move quickly.

Then I hear it: a massive explosion breaking through the water, spewing it up into the air. There is no mistaking what has happened. The bomb has gone off. The sound will travel for miles. I turn to the sea. I don't understand. I left out the third wire. They told us it couldn't blow up without the third wire.

The truck starts behind me. I turn and see Gil through the windscreen. He's tense, the mission isn't complete, but there is jubilation in his eyes; his expression is alight with triumph. I turn back to the water. What have I done?

I watch Tom and Baz run to the truck. I should be following them, but my legs won't move. The sound of that bomb is still in my mind. I left out the third wire, but it exploded. Something starts to shatter inside like I'm a mirror breaking into a thousand shards, my reflection disintegrating. My legs tremble. I thought I had a choice. I didn't. The third wire was never needed, that's what I see. They lied to me. *Gil* lied to me. I have become a Disciple.

CHAPTER 33

Something slams into my back. The force throws me to the ground. I lie there, winded.

I hear Spike. 'Oh, fuck!'

Shots are fired from his direction. I can't move and I'm struggling to breathe. As the seconds pass, I realise I've been shot. Hands suddenly grab at my body, pulling me forward. Tom and Gemma are dragging me back to the truck. My legs struggle beneath me; I know we need to get away. They haul me into the rear of the vehicle, and Tom moves quickly to release my chest from the wetsuit. He assesses the damage.

'It's okay,' he says, sounding relieved. 'It looks like it's gone in the back and come out the front. The bullet's not lodged inside.'

I close my eyes. I don't want to think about it. There is a hole shot through me.

'Move your fingers.' It's Gemma's voice. 'And your feet, your toes.' It takes a lot of effort, but I can move them. 'It missed your spine.'

I hear the doors of the truck slam shut, the thrust of the gear stick, and then we're off, careering away from the coast.

'I'm going to be sick.' I can't get the sentence out before I turn my head and vomit.

'Oh, shit,' Gemma says. I've spewed onto her.

I'm lying flat, aware of increasing pain in my chest, and breathing is no easier. My body is shaking involuntarily; I'm freezing. Something terrible has happened. Gil told me they'd protect me, but I've been shot. The movement of the truck feels jagged beneath me. I concentrate on not being sick again, but I'm afraid. I try to keep my thoughts still, but the pain keeps intruding and the pain makes me frightened.

'How long until we get to hospital?' I think if I can gauge we're getting near, I can hang on. I can keep from cracking. I can stay brave.

'We're not going to hospital,' Tom says matter-of-factly.

Now I know I am in a cruel situation.

'We're going back to the house,' he continues. 'We'll look after you there.'

I swallow. 'I'm in a lot of pain. I need to get to hospital.'

Neither Tom nor Gemma reply. But I need help.

'I don't want to die.'

'None of us want to die.' Tom's voice is vicious. 'And if you hadn't taken so long, we wouldn't be in this mess.' His words sting.

'Tom.' Gemma scolds. 'Jesus.'

'I'm sorry,' he mutters, although he doesn't sound apologetic. Then after a while he continues more gently. 'Listen, Dominic, this is the situation. They're looking for us now, so we're in a compromised position. But when we get back, we'll give you some stuff to make you feel better.'

'I need to get to hospital.' I don't believe they can look after me. He's lying.

'You're not going to hospital. That would be the end of everything, for all of us.'

I think of Gil in the front. He doesn't know what's going on. 'I need to speak to Gil.'

Tom shakes his head. 'Trust me, Dominic. This is as much Gil's command as mine.'

I'm exhausted. The talking has left me empty. There is just pain rattling through my body. I close my eyes again and try not to cry. I think I'm going to die; the possibility feels very real. I don't want it to happen in this truck with these people. I want my sister and Flint.

The vehicle stops. Nobody moves and nobody gets down. I open my eyes and turn to Tom. I hear a helicopter somewhere overhead. Tom places his fingers over his lips, instructing me to stay silent. It's too dangerous to move. The minutes tick by. The beat of the helicopter's rotors seems incessant. Tom and Gemma are absolutely still, hardly breathing, proof of the pressure we're under. The longer we're there, the harder it becomes for me to breathe. I feel increasing panic; the helicopter will never go, and I can't hold out. My breath quickens; it grows louder. Tom's expression is furious in response – he won't have it. Then I'm gasping for air. He moves his hand to gag me, his fingers vice-like across my face. I start to struggle, frantic. A few tears of terror escape my eyes.

Then Gemma's cool hands touch my cheeks gently. She strokes them. It is the first comforting sensation I've experienced in that truck. My struggling lessens. She leans over and kisses me silently on the forehead, then she removes Tom's hand from my mouth. I feel calmer. Tom sits back and my breathing quietens. Gemma keeps her hands on me, stroking my face and hair. She doesn't say a word but comforts me with her touch. I close my eyes. I imagine her hands are Mary's; she'd smile at me and reassure me. I try to keep my thoughts on Mary, and drift into unconsciousness.

Later, I don't know how much later, but I suspect after a long time, we arrive back at the mansion. I wake as they move my body roughly and quickly indoors. There are no lights on but the mood in the house is very tense.

'Bridget, Chloe, gunshot wound,' Gil barks. He's taking command. I know Bridget once trained as a doctor. Some kind of plastic sheeting is thrown across the living room table, and then they lay my body down carefully.

'Everyone else…back to your rooms,' Gil instructs.

I sense people moving slowly; they're curious.

'I said,' he starts to shout, 'back to your rooms!'

'But he's my brother.' Charley's there.

'I don't care who he fucking is,' Gil snarls. 'Get out!'

After a short while, the place grows quiet. Bridget and Chloe come forward to examine me. Gil and Tom stand nearby, watching.

'Okay,' Gil says. 'What's going on?'

'It looks like a clean shot, straight through,' Bridget says. 'I don't think anything vital's been hit, but I can't be sure.'

Gil turns to Tom. I can see they're not happy. I want to speak to Gil, but I feel too weak.

Bridget continues, observing my shaking body. 'Obviously he's in shock and pain…and he's lost some blood.'

'A lot?' Gil asks.

'Enough to be a concern, but we'll manage.'

Gil steps forward, coming to my side. He looks down at me. It's the first contact we've had since I was shot. I see the anger in his eyes.

'I'm…I'm…s-so-rry,' I stutter. I can't bear his disapproval.

He grits his teeth. 'So am I.' I wait for him to say more, something comforting. That they'll get me help, I'll be alright. I need to hear that.

'Okay.' Gil turns back to Bridget. 'Clean him up and make him comfortable.'

He starts to walk away. I can't believe he's walking away. I did my best; I couldn't have swum any faster. The bomb went off, and I didn't mean to get shot.

'Gil.' Somehow I manage to call his name.

He turns to me slowly, waiting for what I've got to say. But I'm silent. I can't speak. I don't want him to be like this, but how do I say that? He turns again and leaves the room.

Finally, alone with Bridget and Chloe, I cry. The pain in my body matches the pain in my mind. But I deserve it. I got so much wrong. The bomb went off; gallon upon gallon of crude oil will be flooding into the sea. I've created an environmental disaster. And still, Gil hates me. Now I know the truth: the Disciples are ruthless and cruel. The worst has happened. They've eaten my soul and I let them do it.

Bridget and Chloe attend to my body quietly. They utter the odd word to each other but otherwise ignore my crying. I watch as Bridget fills a syringe from a vial, tests that the liquid runs through the needle, then gives me a shot in the back of my hand.

She watches my face for a response. 'Better?' she asks.

Whatever she's given me floods my body, taking away the pain. My thoughts jumble; no point trying to think anymore.

'Better,' I acknowledge, because I know now I can sleep, and sleep is oblivion.

I watch as they rig a drip to my left arm and then slip into unconsciousness.

CHAPTER 34

I wake. I'm back in the loft. My eyes slowly focus on Flint; he's watching me. He looks different. I think he's been crying.

'Hey,' he says gently. 'I was wondering when you'd come round.'

My body feels numb. There is a drip in my arm, and I'm lying on some kind of mattress on the floor. I remember what happened. My stomach shifts.

'I'm going to be sick.'

Flint is quick by my side with a plastic bowl. I try to vomit, but nothing comes up. I lie back again. We are quiet for a while.

'Where's Charley?' I eventually ask.

'Downstairs,' he replies. 'I insisted she get some food.'

I feel disorientated. 'What time is it?'

'Six thirty in the evening. You've been out for a while.'

I'm glad he's there. I couldn't bear to be on my own. I feel terrible. 'I messed up, Flint.'

'I guess.' He shrugs. 'They're celebrating downstairs. Apparently, you did better than intended. The bomb was placed further down the pipeline than rehearsed, which blew a bigger hole in it.'

'No,' I mumble, wretched. I remember Tom speaking harshly, asking why I'd taken so long. I must have swum too far, but I swear I used their navigation device correctly. My memory struggles with something else, but I can't grasp it.

'Please don't hate me,' I whisper.

'I'd never hate you, Dom,' Flint says kindly. 'Life's full of mistakes.'

But I saw anger in Gil's eyes. He doesn't accept mistakes. Then, as though he's heard my thoughts, the loft door opens and Gil steps in. He motions for Flint to leave. He comes towards me and I grow afraid.

'How you feeling?' he asks gently.

'Pretty bad.'

'Well, they've pumped you full of painkillers and antibiotics. That should aid your recovery.'

'I'd rather be in hospital,' I tell him.

'No.' He shakes his head. 'Whatever happens, you won't be going to hospital.'

A shiver runs down my spine. I can't contemplate the situation if a bullet had shattered my bones.

'You did well,' he continues more jovially. 'Really well, Dominic. You were a true warrior in the end.' He smiles at me, his words genuine.

I will never understand Gil. 'I thought you were angry with me?'

'No. Although…obviously…I would've preferred you not to have got shot. You took too long. That can't happen again. It meant the blast was greater, but the risk too high.'

My heart sinks. He is already thinking of the next time.

'My soul…' I struggle, but the words won't come.

He looks at me, intrigued. 'What about your soul?'

'You have it,' I whisper. I admit defeat.

Our eyes meet. He is still and calm. 'Rest,' he says. He moves to adjust the blanket gently on me and then leaves the room. It is only when he stands I notice Charley by the door. I do not know what she's heard, but she's always known the truth. She stands there silent, crying.

It is evening again. Dom is deteriorating. He's mumbling in his sleep; he's delirious. Flint thought he'd pull through, he believed it completely, but that was last night. Now, Charley stretches out her hand to feel her brother's temperature again.

'His forehead's burning.' She shakes her head, distressed. She rises and leaves the loft. She barely knows what to do with herself. Flint can see she's gripped by panic and dread. 'Bridget, Gil, somebody help us!' she screams from the top of the stairs. She waits a moment then returns to the loft. She sits by her brother.

Flint can't speak. None of this should be happening.

Bridget comes up and examines Dominic. 'It's not good.' She pauses. She feels his pulse. 'This is what we didn't want to happen.'

'What?' Flint asks, his heart pounding.

'Septicaemia,' Bridget replies gravely. 'His blood's become infected. Shit.'

'And that means what?' Flint says, agitated.

'It means if we don't get the right medication, he could die.' Bridget's words are stark.

The blood drains from Charley's face.

'But we'll get the right medication, won't we?' Flint insists.

'I need to speak to Gil.' Bridget gets up.

'So you'll speak to him immediately,' Flint almost shouts. ''Cause there's no time for some goddamn Disciples discussion about medicines.'

'I'll speak to him immediately,' Bridget replies. She leaves.

Flint and Charley wait. It is taking too long. Then Gil comes up to the loft. He is quiet, his manner subdued. Flint doesn't think he's got anything good to say.

'I'm sorry.' He focuses on Charley. 'But what your brother needs is only available in hospital. And he can't go there.'

Charley gives a brittle half laugh. 'Don't be stupid, he's got to go there.'

Everything is out of control. Flint's about to lose it; he can feel his anger rising.

'Dominic is a young man with a gunshot wound,' Gil says aggressively. 'If he goes to hospital, as soon as he arrives, the police will be informed. They'll realise who he is. And by tomorrow morning, this place will be surrounded, and then it's possible none of us will see the light of day again. *He will not go to hospital.*'

'What are you saying?' Charley asks, breathy, her eyes wide. 'That you're going to let my brother die?'

'I am saying he's not going to hospital,' Gil replies forcefully. 'I will not let him be the death of you, me and everyone else in this house.'

Flint feels rage – pure white fire engulfs him. He flies at Gil. Can't stop himself. He brings Gil down; he's going to punch his head in, he's going to kill him. 'My cousin's done what you wanted,' he shouts. 'You made him a Disciple, you fucking bastard. You got him onside, and now you're going to leave him to die!'

But then Flint's choking. He's pinned under Gil's body; his arm's pressed tight against his throat. Flint had no idea the guy was so strong.

'You have three choices for Dominic,' Gil hisses. 'You control yourself and hear them, or I make the decision for you.'

Charley is shaking, her teeth chattering. Flint stops struggling; they've got to get the best for Dom. Gil slowly takes his arm off Flint's throat. They both stand, and Gil's eyes tell him to step away. Flint takes two paces backwards.

'If you cannot cope with the situation emotionally,' Gil says plainly, 'we shall take Dominic downstairs and look after him until it's over.'

Charley starts moaning, a strange animal sound. He's talking about her brother's death.

Gil is breathing hard; Flint thinks it's possible he cares or he's afraid. 'If you prefer,' Gil continues, 'and you can handle it, we shall leave Dominic here and keep him comfortable. You can stay with him until the end.'

There is a long silence. Gil seems to have finished.

'And the third choice?' Flint asks, his voice hoarse.

Gil draws in a deep breath. 'We end it quickly with a pistol. A bullet to the head, through a pillow. It's not messy that way. It's quick. It's over.'

Charley closes her eyes. She looks sick. Flint is powerless, completely unable to save her from this.

'Dominic entered the world with me,' Charley whispers. She keeps her eyes shut. 'He leaves it that way too, with me by his side.' She opens her eyes but won't look at Gil.

'If you are able to stay calm,' he says softly. 'I will respect your decision.'

He turns to Flint who nods, yes. It's Charley's choice.

'Okay,' Gil agrees. 'Bridget will come up periodically and check on him.'

'And you?' Flint asks, but his anger has gone.

'You may think this an easy decision for me to make. It's not,' Gil responds. 'The last thing I want to do is lose Dominic. But…' He shakes his head. 'I cannot risk everyone else's lives.' He pauses. 'I'm truly sorry.' He leaves the loft.

The silence that follows is the worst that Charley and Flint have known. They understand there is no hope. Dominic is going to die.

CHAPTER 35

I have brief moments of consciousness. I wake. My sister's body is curled up against mine. Flint sits at my side.

'What's happening?' I ask, my throat dry.

Flint is quiet; his eyes are sad.

'Dom,' Charley says softly. 'I love you.'

'Charley.' I choke. *I'm sorry,* I whisper into her head. I don't know what I'm sorry for, but something is wrong. Every part of me knows something is very wrong.

'I love you,' she repeats, into my thoughts. *'I'm sorry too. I never want us to fight again.'*

My eyes open. It's dark. A man's shadow watches over me. 'Dad?' I think it's him, at last.

'No, it's Gil.' His voice is hushed.

'Gil.' I repeat his name. It's a strange name. I've always wondered where it came from.

'It's a Hebrew word,' he tells me. Somehow, he's heard my thoughts. 'It means joy.'

I don't get that. Instead, I remember swimming. Swimming for a long time. 'Fish have gills,' I mutter. Of course, they breathe underwater. 'I want my father,' I tell him. 'I want Dad.' I feel so bad, like I could die. 'Kingfisher.' The word grips me. Dad, wherever you are, that's it. The last word. 'Kingfisher,' I hiss; it takes all my energy to say it. I close my eyes and feel myself sinking.

'Kingfisher?' Gil turns to Flint.

'It's…' Flint stalls. 'It's a long story.' He's not going into it, and never with Gil. None of it matters anyway. Kingfisher is irrelevant, or will be once Dom's dead.

Gil turns to Charley. 'Your father…' he says very quietly, hesitant, 'said that…he thought of you and Dominic as kingfishers. Special and unique. That he saw one as a child and…' He shrugs. There is a long pause. 'I never really understood why he told me that.'

Flint doesn't want to cry, not in front of Gil, but he feels tears on his cheeks. He misses his mum. *Rena, I want you here. I wish everything had turned out differently.*

'Yes,' Charley replies. She must know her father could have said that, but will never know why he told Gil. Still, it is a moment for honesty. 'We are his kingfishers,' she says slowly, 'and you've killed one of us.'

Gil's face seems to twitch with tension. 'Perhaps.' He exhales.

'We'd like you to go now,' Charley says.

Gil nods, gets up and leaves.

The house, for once, is quiet. It is very late. Nobody expects Dominic to be alive in the morning. Charley lies beside him, sobbing gently.

'I can still feel the warmth of his body,' she whispers, but both she and Flint know that won't last for long.

Flint doesn't want to intrude, this is about Charley and Dom, but he feels desperate. He doesn't know how he'll survive if Dom dies. He had no idea he could feel so bad. When Frank died it was awful, but Rena was there. His mother protected him, comforted him. But now…Oh, God, is there really no hope?

'We've got to do something,' he croaks, his throat tight.

Charley looks across at him.

'*You've* got to do something.' He nods at her. He's crying.

'What?' she replies, upset. 'What can I possibly do, Flint?'

'You can't let him die,' he almost wails. 'Dominic cannot die, not here, not like this.'

'Flint, there's nothing we can do,' she says.

'I think you can. *You* can, Charley.' There are things they've never spoken of. 'You've got to do something – like you did that day with the kitten. You can't let Dominic die.'

There is silence. Memories and silence.

'You can save him, Charley,' Flint whispers. 'I believe you can do it.'

She says nothing. She's heard him and stirs. She slowly sits on her knees and puts her shaking hands on Dom's face. It is too pale, like death is already there. She edges his head back gently so his chin is higher than his forehead. She stops, hesitating.

'You can do it, Charley,' Flint insists. It's their only hope.

She leans over and takes a deep breath. Her mouth touches Dom and she releases her breath into him. She waits a moment then repeats the action slowly, breathing into her brother.

The mud in my mind clears. I'm conscious of something, although maybe I'm dreaming. I'm swimming through water, deep down in water. At first it is dark; I can't see properly. But then it starts to brighten. I am swimming through river water. There are ripples of light above; the sun shining on its surface. Bubbles rise from my lips; I watch them. The water is cool against my naked skin. I am at peace, part of the river. Then something dives down, just ahead of me, a flash of azure blue. It has a long, dark beak. It reaches down quickly then rises up, a flicker of fish in its mouth. I follow it, emerging through the water's surface. I breathe. The air is cold, my eyes open.

I wake. There is a female face above me. She has a luminous quality; something sacred about her. She kisses me. Our lips touch softly then she withdraws. My memory shimmers. Her head leans down again and this time I gasp. My sister's hands hold my face. We are still. Nothing moves but our thoughts.

'You're awake, Dom. You're alive.'

'Yes.' I exhale.

'You did it.' Flint comes into view. 'You did it, Charley. I can't believe what I've just seen.' He kneels by me and touches my face, incredulous. 'Dominic?'

'Yes,' I mutter.

'You're still with us.' He swallows.

'Yes.'

My sister puts her hand on Flint's arm, calming him. We are quiet, all three of us, amazed.

'I'm tired,' I eventually tell them.

'Yes,' my sister says. 'It's okay to sleep now.'

'I don't want to die.'

'No,' she promises. 'You're not going to die.'

Gil stands in the loft. The sun streams in through the skylight. His eyes betray how glad he is to see me alive, but he also senses something else.

'How did you do it?' he asks, watching me closely.

'What?' I'm propped up on pillows. I feel very weak.

'Survive,' he says pointedly.

I move my head. 'I don't know.'

He turns to Charley and Flint. 'What happened?'

There is a pause.

'I was lying beside him,' Charley starts, trying to keep her voice even, 'and Flint was over there, and…we cried ourselves to sleep, and when we woke…Dominic was still alive.'

Gil holds her in his gaze. 'And that's all?' He knows something has happened, something incredible.

'That's all,' Charley replies.

He doesn't believe her. I know him well enough to read that.

'Well,' he says slowly. 'It's good. It's very good that you're alive, Dominic.' He smiles. His eyes meet mine. I could believe he cares.

CHAPTER 36

It takes me time to recover. In the weeks that follow, I spend long hours sleeping in the loft, regaining my strength. Flint and Charley are also given space. They don't need us for a while because Operation Gideon was such a success. Gil and Tom keep their distance, but Baz and Gemma come up to me periodically. They try to raise my spirits, although I don't doubt they report back to Gil.

'What can I tell you,' Baz says jovially. He passes me a stash of printouts from the internet. 'Arguments rage, conspiracy theories abound, and Gil is a happy man, as are we all. We're proud of you, Dominic.'

According to the media, a skirmish took place. A LifeStar guard was shot, and it's thought one of us was too. But who we are, and what we were doing, are questions open to speculation. LifeStar Corporation insist the Disciples caused the blow-out, but other voices accuse LifeStar of bucking their responsibilities, seeking a scapegoat for their corporate mistakes. There is a race to save wildlife from the oil slick, and the tide of opinion is turning increasingly against the oil industry; many argue its time is up. All of it confirms Gil's belief: the end justifies the means. But that's not how I see it.

What I've done haunts me. I feel sick most of the time. My thoughts keep returning to what happened that night. I can't stop thinking about the third wire. I know I didn't attach it. I couldn't have; although my memory blurs, I don't believe I would have done it. Yet the bomb exploded. Gallons of crude oil poured into the sea. So what does that mean? What does that make me? I feel the tension of the truth twist inside. At night, I feel most desperate.

'Dom,' Flint whispers through the dark. Tonight, the loft feels stifling. He shuffles over to me, careful not to wake Charley. 'You've got to stop crying.'

I try to swallow a sob.

'They used you, Dom. It's messed you up, but you can't keep crying.' He stretches out his hand. I feel its weight on my chest, warm and heavy where my heart is, comforting.

'We've got to get out of here,' he whispers. 'It's all that matters now. 'Cause we both know they can never find out about Charley.'

I'm quiet. His words slowly sink in. I can never take back what happened, never reverse time, but I can look to the future.

'We have to protect Charley,' I acknowledge.

'Yes, and you know them best. Gil's spent the most time with you. You need to think, carefully, about where there's some place of weakness that will let us escape. They must have a blind spot. We've got to get away.'

I take a few deep breaths, my mood growing calmer.

'Okay?' Flint checks.

I take my time but nod, yes.

'I hate to see you cut up, Dom, but escaping is the only thing that's important now.'

'Yes.' He's right. There is nothing else.

I wake the next morning. The world feels less clouded. For the first time in a long time, I know what to do. I have to confront Gil. He's the only way out.

*

Three weeks later, I watch the snow fall outside. It's thick on the ground. Christmas is approaching but you wouldn't know it here. Christmas, the Disciples insist, is a capitalist construct.

'Once,' Gil explained, 'it was a genuine pagan festival. A celebration of the winter solstice. Then the church stole it from the people and now it's a triumph of capitalist marketing.'

I don't care about Christmas, only getting away. I don't care about the snow because we can't wait until it melts. Finally, I realise, I'm feeling stronger.

I walk down the corridor to Gil's room. I have no idea how what I've got to say will play out, but I'm trusting something deep inside. I haven't told Charley or Flint what I intend to do because they wouldn't get it. I must act alone. The door to Gil's study is open. He is sitting with Tom, some kind of map laid out before them. I knock on the door to register my presence. Both look up.

'I need to speak to you, Gil.' It's a good start; I sound strong. 'Alone.'

There is a brief pause. 'Now's not a good time.' I've never approached him like this before; I don't think he likes it.

'It's important,' I say, 'about Operation Gideon.'

'Then whatever you've got to say, Dominic, can be said in front of Tom too.'

'No.' I shake my head. 'I can only speak to you.'

I sense Tom's hackles rising, and I'm pushing Gil, but I must be on my own with him. Eventually, Gil gives Tom a nod. He gets up and leaves us. I shut the door behind him. I move closer to Gil's desk.

'There's something you need to know,' I start boldly. 'I committed an act of treachery. I left out the third wire.'

Gil grows very still.

'But it didn't matter,' I continue quickly, 'because the bomb exploded anyway, as you always knew it would.'

He takes his time responding. I stand there waiting, the silence full of tension.

'I'm leader of the Disciples,' he says carefully. 'It's my duty to prepare for every eventuality, including the possibility that you wouldn't be as compliant as we needed.' He stops. That's all he says, but his words are like a punch in the chest.

'So you're admitting…the third wire was a set-up?' I don't sound so steady now. For reasons I cannot explain, I feel wounded. 'And all that practice, all that time we spent in agony with our fingers in ice, was irrelevant because the third wire was never needed. You told us a lie.'

Gil's face is impassive. He doesn't seem perturbed in any way by what he's done. But I'm beginning to shake; something inside me is cracking.

'As it happens…the second wire wasn't needed either. But I did need you to plant that bomb.'

I'm winded. I have to sit down. The truth is more terrible than I'd imagined. Charley was right – the only thing we could have done was refuse them. I thought I could sabotage the operation because I was blind to the truth. Blind to what was really happening. Blind to Gil.

'You bastard.' I'm trembling. 'You fucking evil bastard.' The room spins and I'm breathing hard. 'You needed me to plant that bomb.' That's what he said. 'You used me.'

Charley understood, Charley always knew. And Flint couldn't have stated it more clearly. 'That guy's worked hard on you. He's been grooming you from the start.' My mouth is dry. I might be sick.

'You used me,' I repeat. 'And…everything you've said and done…everything…' I realise. 'Was to get me to plant that bomb. To have me onside…enough…to plant that bomb.' I shake my head, distraught. 'Charley and Flint would never have made that mistake.'

'They were more defiant than you,' he acknowledges.

'So I've been the fool, the idiot, because I believed you…what you said…and…' I choke. 'I thought you cared, that something special connected us!'

I'm shaking, struggling with the truth; how complete his victory has been over me. I'm crying, tears of rage and humiliation. I cover my face with my hands. I didn't die from that bullet, but still Gil's killed me. 'You bastard.'

He is quiet for a while. He doesn't even stir. My body shivers, wretched.

'Dominic,' he eventually says, his voice surprisingly soft. 'Do you really believe I'm so calculating and cruel that all I'd do is use you?'

I think of that ride we took on his motorbike. The crazy way he drove, the peace I felt afterwards. It meant something then, but I see it very differently now. 'Yes,' I reply. I won't look at him.

'No. I've had to make choices, difficult operational choices, but that doesn't mean I don't care about you or like you.'

'Gil.' I face him. 'All you do is lie to me. You told me you'd protect me, and I got shot. And then you were prepared to let me die. That's not care.'

He shakes his head. 'That, Dominic, was the most terrible decision I've had to make, but it was the only one I could make. If it had been me who was shot, I'd have insisted Tom do exactly the same. And if you'd died, it would have hurt us, hurt us all, because you're well liked and admired here.'

Suddenly, he sounds so reasonable. He always manages to do that.

'The first time I felt you cared,' I tell him, remembering it clearly, 'was that night you told me your sister died, and you understood how I felt. And that was all a lie too.'

His face pales. He stalls. 'That,' he says very slowly, 'was not a lie.'

Now I grow still. Our eyes meet. He's telling the truth. Everything suddenly jumbles in my mind. We are quiet for a while. Nothing is simple. I need to be brave. I need to trust myself even though I've misjudged so many things.

'Gil,' I say, calmer. My tears have dried up. 'We can't stay here anymore. We're leaving.'

'Dominic, you're a Disciple now,' he replies, equally calm. 'You've committed an act of terrorism. MI5 were looking for you before, and now the stakes are much higher. You're no longer innocent. It's like once you've lost your virginity, you don't get it back. What makes you think you can leave?'

'Because we have to. We must. All three of us know that. We won't stay, whatever the consequences.'

'Dominic, you were shot,' he continues carefully. 'That's a traumatic event. I understand you feel a lot of rage towards me, and the Disciples, for that. But you cannot leave.'

'We can, and we will. Tonight, we're going.'

Gil looks bemused. He doesn't quite know what's going on. That's good.

'I don't think this conversation is useful anymore,' he says. 'You're still recovering, and we should discuss this another time. We can come to an arrangement that feels more comfortable for you. A way of working together.'

He thinks he can negotiate. He's wrong. I stand up to go.

'I don't hate you, Gil,' I say softly, because it's the truth, and I need to hear what he says back.

'No, Dominic.' He sighs. 'And I've never hated you. None of this has been about hate. Quite the opposite.'

I walk out of his room. I know now, we shall be free.

CHAPTER 37

It's late. The house is quiet. Earlier, we heard the usual movement of people below: doors opening and closing, footsteps on the stairs, a few shrieks of laughter. Now, it is quiet. Flint and Charley lie silent and alert in their sleeping bags. I rise from mine.

'We must pack our rucksacks,' I instruct. I told them earlier we're leaving tonight.

'Dom,' Flint says, 'you need to tell us the plan.' He's up and out of his sleeping bag. Charley moves quickly too.

'We're going to walk out of here. All of us, together.'

There is a long pause. Their expressions tell me they don't believe what they've just heard.

'That,' Flint says, 'is not a plan, Dom. It's madness. There are two armed guards downstairs and they will not let us go.'

'Ultimately, they will,' I reply, 'or rather, Gil will let us go.'

'Dom, stop.' Charley's eyes are full of concern. 'What's going on?'

'We have to get out of here. I can't stay here any longer and neither can you. We should have gone long ago, but fear and their tactics stopped us.'

'And the fact they're armed,' Flint points out, 'and there's been no way to escape.'

'But there is now,' I insist. 'Gil's the answer. Gil will let us go.'

Flint shakes his head. 'Gil is a dangerous, ruthless man. He will not let us go.'

'I say he will,' I repeat. 'I need you to trust me on this. Deep down, in the depth of my being, I know he will let us go.'

'No, Dom,' Charley says. 'You don't. He'll kill you.'

A tense silence spreads between us.

'He's already done that, Charley.' I struggle. 'He got me to plant that bomb, he turned me into a Disciple. I can never change that. But I will not give him my future, and if I stay here…he'll have it. He'll win.'

Neither of them argue with that.

'Gil pushes everything to its limit,' I continue. 'He practically pushed me over it. But it's the language he understands. And now…I'm going to speak to him in his language. Then he'll let us go.' I stop and swallow. 'The important thing for you is that you make it out quickly, get into one of those trucks and start the engine. Do you think you can do that, Flint?'

He looks at me a long moment. I know he's finding it hard to trust me on this.

'They don't always lock the doors,' I point out.

'No,' he agrees. 'I've noticed that. And…they're old vehicles. The wires should be exposed. Once inside, it should be easy to start.' He sounds cautious, but I think he's onside.

'The snow's thick on the ground,' Charley protests.

'Yes,' I say, 'but they've still been using those trucks. The roads aren't impassable yet, so while you two get into a truck, I'll deal with Gil.'

'No,' Charley fires back. 'No, Dom. You can't do this. He'll kill you. I've saved your life once, I can't do it again. You stop, now. Tell him, Flint. Tell him he can't do this.'

Flint is quiet. His eyes meet mine.

'Today is a good day to die,' I say. He doesn't respond, not immediately, but it's a phrase I looked up in the library here.

A Native American phrase one their warriors followed. I think he'll get it.

'Yeah.' He eventually nods. 'Today is a good day to die.'

Charley's face pales.

'*Charley,*' I whisper into her head. '*Kingfishers need to be free. They're not captive animals.*' I can see the anguish behind her eyes. 'We can't stay here,' I tell her aloud. 'You know that.'

'I don't want you to do this.'

'I know. But we have to. I wish things were different too, but they're not.'

She grows still. I wait, then she nods.

We stop talking, pack our rucksacks and pull them onto our shoulders. We come together for a final hug, then we slip out of the loft and start down the stairs. When we reach the main communal living room, it isn't immediately apparent if anyone is there. It's shrouded in darkness, and the guards patrol the whole house. If we're in luck, maybe they won't find us. The kitchen is towards the back with a side door off it. The trucks should be outside that door. We start to cross the room carefully.

'What are you doing?' We're not alone. It's Taylor; he's on duty tonight.

'We're leaving,' I say as coolly as I can.

He steps forward and raises his gun. 'No way.' He motions for us to move back. 'Spike,' he calls out, 'I need you in here.'

Spike comes quickly. He looks at us suspiciously. 'I'll go get Gil.'

'I'm already here,' Gil's voice tells them. Although the kitchen is in shadow, he's standing there.

'What would you like us to do?' Taylor asks, sounding surprised he hadn't noticed Gil before. None of us did. But he knew what we would do, what *I* would do, and he's been waiting. It's a good sign. It shows how much we understand each other.

'Go and patrol the front of the house,' Gil orders. 'I'll deal with them.'

They start to leave, but Spike hesitates before Gil. He nods to them, and they go. Once we're alone, Gil steps forward out of the shadow. He's pointing a pistol at us.

'Outside.' He motions to the door. We hesitate, nervous. 'Outside,' he commands. 'That is where you want to go.'

Gil's eyes focus on me. I step very slowly backwards, never taking my eyes off his. Charley and Flint pass quickly out the side door; I hear their feet running. Gil and I edge out after them. I dare to glance briefly behind. Charley and Flint open the doors to one of the trucks. They disappear inside. I feel a light-headed relief, but then hear a shot. It ricochets off the bumper. I turn back to face Gil and place my body in front of his gun.

'Don't shoot them,' I say with as much control as I can. 'They won't go without me.'

'Of course not. They'll be around to bury your body.'

We stand opposite each other, so close his pistol touches my chest. I can't quite believe what's happening, what I'm doing.

'You need to let us go, Gil.' I feel sick.

'I don't need to let you do anything.'

'We're going. You either give us our freedom or you shoot me.' Everything seems unreal. I'm breathing fast – he'll know I'm afraid.

'Suddenly, you're ready to die?' he says, but his voice sounds altered. This is difficult for both of us.

'You've had my life twice,' I continue, hoarse with tension. 'You took it that first night you almost drowned me, and you had it when I was shot. Now give me it back. Set me free. It's what you believe in, isn't it? Freedom?'

'You know I can't let you go,' he says, shaking his head.

'You can, Gil. You're the only one who can.'

He's so close, I can smell the sweat on his body. I think we're like wild animals, charged with fear and ready to attack.

'Let me go, or shoot me.' I hope he can't see me trembling. 'If I can't be free, I'd rather be dead.'

Behind us, the truck kicks into life. Flint has managed to start it. Gil suddenly grabs the back of my head, pulling my hair, drawing me closer to him. He shoves the pistol under my chin; his arms are shaking with tension.

'Set me free,' I mutter through clenched teeth, 'or shoot me.' I'm about to vomit and I don't know if I can control the piss in my bladder. Gil's breath quickens. I sense his strength; there is no way I can fight him off.

'Set me free,' I whisper. He pulls my head back hard, my neck suffering, and I cry out in pain. My knees buckle under me and I'm staring up into his face. He puts the gun, deadly and cold, against my forehead.

I hear the door of the truck open. I guess it's Flint. I want to call out, to tell him to stay back, but I can't. The moment is desperate. Gil's expression is terrifying.

All warmth has died in his eyes – he's become demonic. And I realise I'm going to die. This is the price I pay. Flint and Charley will get away, but I'm going to die. I feel the heat of my own urine flush down my leg. He preps the pistol.

'Gil.' I watch for his finger pulling back on the trigger, my whole body shaking. 'Gil,' I cry; his name will be the last word on my lips.

He looks into my eyes. I don't know what he sees. I'm an exhausted animal at the end of the hunt. The seconds last forever. Then he closes his eyes. A deep growl issues from his body like he's in pain. A shudder courses through him. Finally, he lowers the pistol. He pulls me back up onto my feet, and our bodies lean into each other. We are silent; there is only the strained rasp of our breaths in the night.

Gil swallows. He moves the pistol in his hand, pulls at the top of my jeans, and I feel the cold, hard metal of the gun against me. He withdraws his hand. It's mine.

'Go,' he whispers.

I can't move.

'Turn left at the main road.' It sounds difficult for him to speak. 'Keep driving south and leave the truck back at Gregory's cottage.'

I'm silent, listening to what he's saying, but also to what he's not saying.

'And don't get caught.'

'We won't get caught,' I promise. Still, I can't move. I need to turn quickly and get into that truck. But I hesitate. This will be the last I see of Gil.

'Go,' he insists. 'Go, Dominic, before I change my mind.'

I look into his face for the final time. His eyes are fire. I will never know anyone like him. I turn quickly and run towards the truck. Flint gets back inside; I jump in beside my sister. Flint puts the gear stick into first then forces the truck forward quickly, shifts the gear into second, third, and we're away.

We don't talk, not immediately. The shock of freedom has numbed our minds. The road ahead is dark and empty, snow on either side. We'll be driving a while. I remove the pistol carefully from my jeans and rest it on the dashboard. I hope we never have to use it, but maybe we will. Every second the wheels roll over the tarmac and slush, we're moving further away from the Disciples and Gil. My limbs shake slightly, and I can smell the piss on my clothes.

'You pulled it off,' Flint says in a hushed voice. 'You did it.'

'You need to stop the truck a minute.' My stomach shifts.

Flint brings it to a halt. I get down and vomit at the side of the road. I can't stop the shaking in my body. I stay crouched low and try to still myself.

'Here.' It's Charley. I turn to her. She's standing near me, holding out a clean pair of jeans. It's bitterly cold, but I strip out of my old ones and put on the new.

'You did it, Dom.' She smiles, proud of me. 'We're free.'

'Yeah.'

We get back inside the truck and continue south. I close my eyes and rest my head back, but my body won't stop shivering.

'I've never known anything as brave as what you did,' Flint says gently. Charley moves her warm hand to mine. She squeezes it.

Behind my eyes, the images shift. I'm on that hill with Gil again. It's my seventeenth birthday. We are alone. The night is cold, the sky immense, the stars bright. We move to get back on his bike.

'If nothing else, Dominic,' he says clearly. 'I'll teach you courage.'

I didn't answer him then. But now I feel the tears behind my closed eyes.

'Yes,' I tell him, in the silence of my mind, 'you did that.'

CHAPTER 38

We pull up outside Gregory's cottage. It's shrouded in darkness. No one inhabits it now.

'I was a different person when we were here,' Charley says.

'Yes.' I agree.

'We thought we were safe.' Flint sighs. He shakes his head gently. 'I won't make that mistake again.'

We are quiet for a while.

'Where to next?' Charley asks.

'London,' I reply, surprised at how sure I sound about it. 'It's not home anymore, never will be, but, like Flint said, we can lose ourselves there.'

Neither of them argues with my suggestion.

'We need new transport,' Flint points out. 'We could risk the train, but I'd prefer another vehicle.' He pauses. 'Something like… Gregory's pickup truck.'

I grow still.

'Do you think you could get it through Mary?'

I remember the last time Mary and I met. The sex we had. She's special to me; I'm not sure I want to involve her. I take my time responding.

'We probably could,' I say, 'but…I don't want to do that unless I'm offering to take her with us.'

They are silent. I sense their discomfort at the suggestion. Flint taps the steering wheel softly with his fingers. 'Let's just think about this,' he suggests. 'It's still dark. We're not doing anything for a while.'

I rest my head against the window. I'm exhausted, now the adrenalin that got me through the night has drained away.

'You've been lonely, Dom,' Charley says, and I know she's acknowledging her relationship with Flint. What it's given her, but taken from me. I keep staring into the darkness.

'We're going to London,' Flint says matter-of-factly. 'It's a huge, anonymous city. All Mary knows is this small part of Scotland.' He pauses. 'We can't tell her she'll be safe, 'cause we're not. We can't offer any kind of future 'cause we don't know what it is.'

'When you look at it practically,' I say, 'it would be the maddest, craziest thing for her to do, to join us, but…I want to make that offer. I love her, and it feels the right thing to do.'

'It may not be an offer she accepts,' Flint says carefully.

'No,' I acknowledge. 'She might say no. But at least it will be her choice. Not Gregory's, not the Disciples', just Mary's choice.' I'm upset, because I realise Flint is right.

'I think you should ask her,' Charley says. 'Be honest and truthful, and then if she comes, she's really with us.'

I turn to her. She nods and smiles.

'Yeah,' I say.

Flint nods too, and then we're quiet.

We rest a while, but none of us is able to sleep. Too much has happened, too much is still going on. Flint takes the opportunity to examine the gun. It's fully loaded.

'Shit.' I shudder. Gil was acting with intent. He could have killed me.

'I reckon, if we need to, we can get more ammunition in London,' Flint says.

'I think we should lose it now,' Charley responds. 'It's not like we know how to use it.'

'We know how to use it,' Flint corrects her, 'but that's different to whether we want to.'

'We keep it,' I tell them firmly. 'Gil gave me it because he knows what he's done. He made me a Disciple. He doesn't want us to get caught because they'll be done for too.'

They look at me, slightly shocked.

'I'm just saying,' I continue, a little calmer, 'we can't get caught. I think we hold on to it…at least for the moment.' I don't want to discuss it anymore.

Eventually, the sun rises. We start the long trek back to the village. Flint and Charley agree to occupy themselves while I speak to Mary. The thought of seeing her again fills me with joy. I'm happy being a part of the world she belongs to. I can shift the fear and loneliness that have weighed me down.

Gregory's store is one in a parade of shops. I notice the Christmas lights and decorations; it's another universe from the one we've been in. Behind the shops, there is a parking area. I recognise the pickup truck and linger by it. I don't want Gregory to see me. I wait there observing their back door. It's open; they're probably expecting a delivery. In time, Mary appears. She's hauling some boxes. She doesn't see me. My instinct is to whistle, but of course she won't hear it. Instead, I'm forced to walk over. She looks up and I stop. It takes a few moments for her to fully comprehend it's me, and then she runs over. Without saying a word, we embrace. Her arms are around me and my heart is flying. I hold her tightly, breathing in the sweet smell of her hair and skin, and then we let go.

'We're leaving,' I tell her. I know I can't hesitate or delay. 'And I need to ask you a favour. We need the pickup truck.'

She is still. My words are blunt; they're not coming out like I want.

'We're going to London,' I continue quickly, 'and although I can't promise you anything, I can't even guarantee your safety, if you'd like to come too, then join us.' I'm speaking too fast, I hope she can lip-read what I'm saying. 'I'd like you to come away with us,' I confirm more slowly.

She takes my arm and moves me round the back of the truck. I touch her lips and notice that my hand is trembling.

'I've imagined this moment so many times,' she says, 'you coming to get me.' She looks into my eyes and hers grow moist.

'Yes?'

'Yes.' She swallows. 'I've always imagined…running away with you. Getting away from here.' She pauses.

'Yes,' I repeat. 'I want you to come.'

Her eyes hold mine, but it's as if she's searching for something there. Her breath quickens, and I sense she feels under pressure.

'Only now that you're really here…' She trails off.

My heart starts sinking. She's not going to be able to do it. I'm asking too much. 'It's hard.' I struggle. 'When it's real.' I know I may not be the best thing for her, but that doesn't make me feel any better.

She nods, her lower lip beginning to tremble.

'And we need to leave now,' I tell her. 'We can't stick around, it's too dangerous.'

She nods again. Her eyes fill with tears. I sense this isn't how she thought it would be, however she imagined getting her freedom and away from here. I'm asking her to leave everything she knows.

'I don't know if I can do it.' A few tears trickle down her face. The distance between us widens.

'It's okay,' I say, although it feels difficult to speak. 'You must do what's right for you, Mary. You can't make a mistake. There would be no turning back.' I try to sound reasonable, but I don't feel it.

'I don't know why, but it feels too difficult a decision.'

'Then you must stay.' I have to accept it, although a deep sadness opens up inside me. She cries more easily now, the tears streaking her face.

'We had something special together,' I whisper, 'and…nobody can take that away from us. It belongs in our memories, and in our hearts.' I touch my chest.

She nods, yes. Then we kiss. A final, hot kiss. I don't want to let her go, but I must. 'I will miss you, Mary.' We separate. I want to go, quickly, before the hurt sets in, but we're not finished.

'We…we need the pickup truck,' I remind her. She glances back towards her father's store.

'Meet me in an hour.' She hiccups, wiping away the tears on her cheeks. 'Dad will think I'm doing a delivery.' She pauses and takes a tissue from her pocket. 'I'll give you the keys and some stuff for the journey.' We both know she will have to think up a story for her father. 'I won't let him contact the police.'

'Thank you.' She will be lonely with what she has to do, and so will I.

'I'll meet you near the bus stop on the road leading out of the village.' She is already walking away from me, back to her father's shop.

CHAPTER 39

I find Flint and Charley in the pub car park. I can see their dismay; I'm returning on foot and not in the truck.

'What happened?' Flint asks, concerned.

'Don't worry. We'll get the truck in an hour.'

'An hour?' my sister says, anxious.

'An hour,' I repeat. 'Mary will bring us the truck in an hour. I know she'll keep her word.'

They grow a little calmer. We're going to get to London.

'And…what about Mary?' Flint asks.

'She's not coming.'

Neither of them responds immediately. 'I'm sorry,' Charley says.

'Me too. I need to be on my own a while.'

I can't say anymore, and I can't bear to be with them. I walk towards the trees at the back of the car park. They don't follow. I rest my head against one of them, pressing my forehead into the bark. There were times with the Disciples when thinking of Mary helped me pull through. Now I have to let it all go. What will I draw on for happiness? We hadn't known each other long, yet the connection felt fierce.

'I know the colour of your soul.' I hear her voice again in my mind.

I let out a low, deep moan of grief and crouch down by the tree. I don't know how I'm meant to go on. My heart sobs, but my tears are frozen. I'm so tired, I've had enough.

'Dominic.' Flint touches my shoulder. I didn't hear him approach. He crouches down bedside me. 'I'm sorry. I know it hurts,' he says gently. 'I know it hurts real bad.' He doesn't try to comfort me further, he offers no platitudes; I feel relief at that. He's just said it as it is. He stays with me a while, but we don't say any more. Finally, though, he motions to his watch; we need to go if we're going to meet Mary. We get up and walk back towards my sister. I can see she's upset for me, but she holds her tongue. Words aren't much use now. I shake out my body, trying to shift my mood. We've got a long journey ahead.

We walk towards the arranged meeting place and wait. True to her word, an hour after our discussion, we watch Gregory's pickup truck come towards us. It draws to a halt. Mary looks strained and serious in the driver's seat. She gets down and looks at us. This is goodbye; she'll be left having to concoct a story for her father. I don't envy her that, but she's doing it for me. She takes my hand and walks me a little way from Flint and Charley. There is something final she wishes to say. We stand close to each other. She's breathing quickly, nervous.

'I've got my rucksack in the truck,' she whispers.

I close my eyes a moment. I think I know what she's saying. I try to control the leap in my heart.

'Mary, are you really sure?'

'I'm not sure of anything, except I can't bear that I'll never see you again.' She pauses, her body shaking slightly. 'I don't want you to go without me.'

I draw her towards me and hug her tight, squeezing her body into mine. 'I won't go without you,' I promise.

She lets out a few shocked sobs. She's coming with us; we'll be together. She's breaking away and it's difficult and frightening, but she'll do it for me. I take her face in my hands and kiss her, at first gently and then more passionately. Something in me grows lighter, like it has wings. We release our embrace and I take her hand in mine.

We walk back towards the truck. Charley and Flint realise what's happening. They come over to join us. I take the keys from Mary and throw them to Flint; he can drive a while. I need to hold Mary. My sister smiles. We all squeeze into the truck. Flint starts the engine and throws it into gear. We move off. We've made it this far, and I'm alive. I hold Mary in my arms, her body soft and warm against mine.

ACKNOWLEDGEMENTS

Kingfisher has been an act of faith in itself. It took a lot of writing over many drafts, and in particular I would like to acknowledge the following for their help:

My parents, Arline and Jack, who from a very early age encouraged my writing and believed in me. Thank you for your patience.

Thank you to the Cohen twins for being who you are and sparking my imagination.

Thank you to my editor, Lesley Jones, whose kind encouragement allowed me to take on board all her professional advice, and make the many necessary changes. Your help has been invaluable.

And, last but not least, thank you to Paul for listening to it aloud, providing dramatic insight, but most of all, for your love and support.